The CATE CARLISLE Files

Creating and writing Cate Carlisle has been one of the most exciting experiences of my life. I've tried to write novels before, but somehow nothing quite worked.

As soon as I thought of Cate though, I knew exactly what she would be like. She would be feisty but not bolshy, friendly but not a blabbermouth, fluent in several languages, well travelled, independent and practical. All that I wished I had been as a teenager but wasn't!

I made a resolve that the Cate Carlisle Files would always be about glamour, sunshine, cool people and fabulous locations. I wanted you, the reader, to have some fun, some escapism from our dodgy weather and sometimes endless school work. But I also wanted to open up your eyes to the amazing world out there. So *Trapped* is set on a yacht in the South of France, and the next adventure is in Australia.

I hope you enjoy reading about Cate and that she inspires you to enjoy our world.

Isla Whitcroft

To Eloise,

Have fun with QUE!

Keep writing.

Best wishes,

Jane Morris

July 2012

TRAPPED

ISLA WHITCROFT

PICCADILLY PRESS • LONDON

To my father John Whitcroft (Janek Witkowski),
a man of great spirit who never gave up

First published in Great Britain in 2011
by Piccadilly Press Ltd,
5 Castle Road, London NW1 8PR
www.piccadillypress.co.uk

A catalogue record for this book is available
from the British Library

ISBN: 978 1 84812 154 6 (paperback)

1 3 5 7 9 10 8 6 4 2

Printed in the UK by CPI Bookmarque Ltd,
Croydon, CR1 4PD
Cover design by Simon Davis
Cover illustration by Sue Hellard

PROLOGUE

Deep down, below sea level, was a room so secret that only five people in the entire world knew of its existence. Carefully regulated artificial daylight, air supply and temperature made it perfect for long-term survival and indeed the walls of the room were lined with animal cages of varying sizes, stacked high on top of one another.

Through the wire mesh and steel bars at least twenty pairs of eyes stared out into the sterile environment. They looked angry, resigned or unbearably sad while above them video cameras placed at intervals on the ceiling clicked and gyrated, checking into every corner and crevice of the room.

For these were no ordinary household creatures. Each was from a highly protected species. In one cage, a white lion paced up and down in its cramped space, in another, an orang-utan endlessly counted the fingers on its hairy hands. A Sumatran tiger, an Iberian lynx and a giant panda were also trapped in the endless hell, where water came through a tube and food was scarce.

There was something else notable about the animals: they were all young. The tiger still had the fluffy cuteness of a cub and the orang-utan had yet to develop its powerful limbs and terrifying roar. But the energy and the playfulness of young creatures were non-existent. And their eyes – their eyes seemed to be those of much older animals.

Now the mountain gorilla was staring at something. In a large cage near the sliding doors an object was stirring. But this wasn't an animal – it was a human.

The gorilla suddenly stood up in the cage and screamed in rage and frustration, jolting the other creatures out of their stupor. Within seconds, the room was filled with cries and howls and squawks of protest and panic. The clamour reached through the fuzziness that was swirling around inside the human's head.

A hand slowly felt around, trying to gauge the surroundings, and came up almost immediately against the coldness of a metal bar. Using it as a support, the human slowly and painfully managed to drag itself up into a sitting position.

It was a girl of no more than sixteen, with matted hair and tanned skin. Underneath her tan she was pale, and an injury had left congealed blood dried in a random mess around her forehead. Her throat felt as if it had been burnt with acid and she licked her bone-dry lips. She gagged and spat saliva out. Then, spotting a water drip in the corner of the cage, she dragged herself over to it and placed her mouth under the tube, grateful for the small drops that fell agonisingly slowly down into her parched mouth.

Suddenly the animals went quiet and moved to the back of their cages. The girl was at first too busy to notice but, as the silence sunk into her consciousness, she stopped. With a feeling of dread, she heard footsteps getting louder and louder. She could hear the click of high heels and the more powerful thud of a heavy man's shoes hitting the ground. There was the subdued whoosh of electronic doors sliding open and then the girl could see two sets of legs – one male and one female – standing in front of her cage.

'Well, well,' said the man in a Russian accent. 'And just what new and amazing species do we have here?'

CHAPTER 1

As far as the eye could see there were boats – billions and billions of pounds' worth of boats. Large glistening hulls in every imaginable shade of white, cream and blue swayed in the sparkling water.

The early morning Mediterranean breeze blew in quiet fits and starts and, every now and again, the great gleaming giants strained against their thick ropes in a futile attempt to break free.

Uniformed staff swarmed around each of these huge boats. Handsome men with tough bodies and sun-bleached hair hosed down already immaculate wooden decks. Fit young women in tight denim cut-offs and impossibly white T-shirts buffed gleaming brasswork and French-polished handrails.

Every so often yet another small van would pull up by a gangway, dropping off vast hampers of luxury food, or gleaming spare parts for the massive fuel-hungry engines that lay below deck.

All the while the banter between the people on the boats went on, in French, in Spanish and in English spoken with Australian, South African and American accents. There was laughter and shouting, teasing and flirting. To Cate, as she stood staring, it seemed as if she had suddenly been given access to another world – a world of beautiful people, easy living and wealth beyond measure. Right now, more than anything, Cate wanted in some way – any way – to be part of it.

It was amazing to think that just a few hundred miles away, at this very moment, her friends would be waking up to another grey English day.

Cate looked down at the print-out in her hands. It had been her most prized possession since she had received the email two weeks before, from her father.

Darling Cate,

Charlie, my old friend who runs a yacht agency in Antibes, says that he has found someone who is mad enough to take you on for the summer. Go to berth number 694, Antibes marina, any morning in the last week of June. And I've promised Monique that you will be back at school in September. Don't let me down or I'll never hear the end of it. Stay sensible, trust your instincts and send us an email sometime.

Love you and good luck,
Dad

The email made Cate smile. It was so like her father – kind, straight to the point and determined not to be too controlling of his only daughter.

Seven years before, Cate's mother had left the three of them – Dad, Cate and her brother Arthur – to follow her spirit wherever it took her, which finally turned out to be LA and a variety of weird and wonderful cults and crazies. Cate's dad, a high-flying diplomat had, without fuss, swept Cate and Arthur off to a world of foreign countries, new languages, tutors and as much love and affection as he had time to give.

Luckily Cate had thrived on the organised chaos and constant stimulation that had made up her new life. She had adored living out of a suitcase, never tired of airports and working out strange currencies and felt proud to be part of the close-knit community of ex-pats who always looked out for each other.

There were summer holidays in America staying with their mother and Christmases skiing in Switzerland with their father and, as a result, she considered herself to be an international girl who felt as at home in Lyon as she did in La Paz.

And now, after catching the late night Eurostar from St Pancras, then the early morning TGV from Paris, here Cate was, in one of the most beautiful towns, on one of the most stunning coastlines in Europe, breathing the salt-scented air in excitement.

She pushed her gold-rimmed Ray-Bans – a last minute present from her father's long-term girlfriend, Monique – up on top of her dark blond hair. 'This is it,' she said to herself. 'Time for an adventure.'

Glancing at the numbers painted onto the slatted wooden pontoons, Cate set out on the curved walkway towards the far end of the marina, away from the looming medieval walls built to protect the port from invaders.

As the berth numbers rose to five then six hundred, Cate turned off the concrete walkway onto the pontoons. Through her light flip flops she could feel the warmth of the wood, already heated by the sun. Another few hours and it would be almost too hot to tread on without the protection of thick soles.

Just as she was about to run out of walkway, Cate finally arrived at berth 694 and looked up at the boat. *Catwalk II* was beautiful. The jade green hull was topped with dark polished woodwork and a pure white three-decked stern. The brass fittings sparkled in the sunshine and, through the large glass door, Cate could see luxurious sofas edged around a large salon. A wooden walkway with a rope handle was slung at a sharp angle between the middle deck and the pontoon and, at its foot, stood a big, round basket full of deck shoes.

The boat was twenty-five metres from stern to nose, but seemed devoid of life. While Cate tried to decide whether to call out or simply walk on board, a tall, almost boyishly thin, young woman appeared at the top of the gangway. She had a large straight nose on which rested an enormous pair of sunglasses and her dark hair was tied up with a scarf. She looked Cate up and down, taking in her dusty footwear, her crumpled cut-off cotton trousers, her dirty white shirt and her rather battered suitcase.

'Yes?' she said. The tone was not unfriendly.

'My name is Cate – Cate Carlisle,' said Cate, trying not to sound intimidated. 'I was given the number of this berth by Charlie Summers. He said you were looking for help. He should have told you about me . . .' Cate's voice trailed off in the other woman's silence. Had her dad and Charlie got their wires crossed?

To her relief the woman suddenly smiled. 'Typical Charlie,' she said in a South African accent. 'We do need crew but he never mentioned that he was sending someone. Good job we hadn't hired in the meantime. You'd better come aboard.' She nodded towards the basket. 'Ditch the footwear and choose a pair of deckies. Rule number one of sailing: you can't come aboard in shoes with soles and, worst of all, heels. If you do, the captain will throw you straight back down the gangplank.'

Cate rummaged in the basket for a pair of size sixes. Luckily almost the first pair she picked out fitted perfectly, the expensive tan leather lying like silky slippers around her feet.

She picked up her flip flops, her suitcase and her precious Mulberry rucksack that had seen her through many an adventure and took her first step on board *Catwalk II*. This would be home, she hoped, for at least the next eight weeks.

'You'll have to talk to the captain,' said the woman, as if she was reading her mind, 'but later – he's downstairs working on the engine and must not be disturbed.' She suddenly grinned sardonically and Cate warmed to her. 'I'll show you around in the meantime. I hope you're not afraid of hard work.'

As they walked through the glass doors into the interior of the middle deck, Cate gazed at the utter luxury around her. The middle deck salon was a good five metres square, kitted out almost entirely in cream leather and polished wood. The last time Cate had felt carpet pile this deep was when her dad had taken her and Arthur to the safety of the French Embassy in Damascus after a particular nasty demonstration against the occupation of Iraq had got out of hand.

At the front, on the bridge, a bank of computer screens was blinking and flashing next to a huge nautical steering wheel. An adjustable leather seat was lined up next to the wheel and the view through the sparkling glass window was vast.

In the centre of the salon, several individual seats and sofas were scattered around a wooden block which housed a sink, a fridge and a cabinet with a huge selection of crystal glasses. There was a massive flat-screen TV on the wall and Cate spotted several speakers discreetly built into the furnishings.

'This is where we do the evening and the wet weather entertaining,' the woman explained. 'If the weather is good, the guests prefer to be on the top deck.'

She gestured towards a small spiral staircase in the far corner. They climbed the tiny steps and came out into the sunshine. Wooden sun loungers were invitingly laid out next to a bubbling jacuzzi and small crescent-shaped splash pool. Marble-topped bar stools were submerged into the bright blue water and within arm's reach of the pool was a fully fitted, fully stocked bar. Beyond that stood an LED TV and the slimmest music centre that Cate had ever seen. It was the ultimate rich man's playground. For a few seconds Cate was stunned by it all. Then the woman finally held out her hand.

'I'm Wendy, Wendy Bloemfeld. I'm the steward on board, in charge of housekeeping, entertaining and generally keeping everyone happy. As well as me, there is Marcus the chef and Bill, our illustrious captain, who you'll see in a minute.'

Cate took Wendy's hand and shook it firmly. 'Thanks,' she said. 'Wendy, Charlie didn't quite explain —'

'I need a general dogsbody,' said Wendy. Mind-reading seemed to be a particular skill of hers. 'Someone to make the beds, take the laundry to be washed, clean up after the guests and, if I think you're up to it, stand in for me so I can have a bit of time off the boat.

'Usually we're quiet, but when the boss decides to turn up it's all systems go for as long as she stays. It could be for a day or a month and we don't get any notice. And when she is here – well, don't expect much time off and be prepared for anything.'

Cate was impressed by Wendy. Although probably only in her mid-twenties, she had the no-nonsense air of someone who could cope with most situations.

They headed back down the staircase. On the middle deck they walked through the boarding area of the boat and down a wide, carpeted set of steps into the lower salon. Wendy pushed open the large double doors and Cate took a deep breath. The wood-panelled salon was even more impressive than the one above. The carpet was thick and deep, the jade and cream sofas and chairs liberally strewn with plump cushions. Crystal wall lights provided daylight-level brightness.

At the far end of the room a door was open. 'The master bedroom,' said Wendy, following Cate's gaze. The master suite was bigger than the sitting room in Cate's house in London and was decorated in scarlet and green. There was a marble fireplace in the corner and mock candle lights flickered and stuttered, illuminating the heart-shaped double bed, the floor-to-ceiling closets and the bathroom fashioned almost entirely out of marble. It could have looked tacky, but instead felt sumptuous. At a discreet distance from this room, but also off the main salon, were four large ensuite guest bedrooms.

'Don't get too excited,' said Wendy. 'We get a bunk and a basic bathroom down in the crew quarters.'

Cate suddenly felt a pang of homesickness for her messy, comfortable home and the familiar faces of her family and her best friend Louisa, who she'd met on her first day of school and been practically inseparable from since.

She took a grip of herself. She and Wendy grinned at each other.

'Bill should be just about finishing up now,' said Wendy.

Down in the bowels of the boat, the huge twin engines gleamed, a twisted labyrinth of pipes and blocks and pumps. To Cate's eye, the whole thing seemed an unintelligible mass of metal but clearly the man with his back to her, wiping his hands on a rag, had no such problem. He was tall with broad shoulders and a shock of blond hair. As he heard them approaching, he turned slowly around.

'Bill, this is Cate. She's looking for work as a deckhand and can start today. Charlie sent her.'

There was silence while Bill looked Cate up and down with his piercing blue eyes. Finally he spoke in an Aussie accent. 'Bit young, aren't you?'

'I'm old enough to work.' Inside Cate felt her stomach curling but she forced herself to sound steady.

'Hmm. We're not bloody interested in anyone with trouble behind them. Not running away from anything, are you?'

Cate grinned then. 'Not unless you count exam results,' she said, and saw the beginning of a smile on his handsome face. She took a deep breath and went for it. 'Look, Bill, I love boats, I need a summer job. I'm used to travelling, fending for myself and I hate trouble. If you want to check me out, why not ask Charlie? His office is in town.'

'I know where Charlie is,' said Bill shortly. There was another silence before he turned to Wendy. 'Well, she seems all right to me.' He spoke as if Cate wasn't there. 'But you're the one who will be telling her what to do. Whaddya think?'

Cate held her breath.

'I've seen a lot worse,' said Wendy. 'She doesn't rabbit on for a start.'

It was time to play her trump card.

'I can speak a few languages,' she said brightly. 'That might come in handy.'

'What languages?' said Bill, still looking at Wendy.

'Well, er, French, Spanish, Russian, some Italian and even a bit of Dutch.' Cate decided to leave out Arabic and Mandarin in case it sounded as if she was boasting. 'Like I said, I've travelled a bit.'

When Cate had reached fourteen her father decided that she needed to be at school for her GCSEs and that it was time for her and Arthur to settle in one place. Cate was devastated, and even more so when he ignored her suggestions of somewhere glamorous like Barcelona in favour of a three-storey town house in a quiet street in South Kensington in London.

It wasn't until Monique, a sassy Dutch translator, volunteered to stay with her and Arthur that Cate realised he really did have their best interests at heart and gave in gracefully.

There were compensations for this more ordinary life. For a start, Monique, a black belt in martial arts, was passionate about teaching Cate and Arthur those skills. She also taught the children languages and insisted they spoke a different one at home every day of the week to add to the ones they had already picked up on their travels.

Now she offered up a silent prayer of thanks to her.

'Blimey, mate,' said Bill. 'Impressive. I can only speak Australian!' He nodded to himself. 'You need to know our rules,' he continued. 'I'm captain of this boat and that means everyone – and I mean everyone – has to do as I say, particularly when we're at sea. Lives can depend on it. Got it?'

Cate nodded. She got it.

'Wendy will explain your duties, but there is one thing you need to know right from the off. On this boat there is no such thing as regular hours. When the boss isn't here we can relax a little. There's just maintenance and security and keeping the place ready. Then you get plenty of shore leave. But when she's here, well, it's the opposite. No matter what time of day or night, you're here on this boat on call to her every whim and wish. She pays our wages and owns this boat, and when she gets here she expects the best. The best service, the best comfort, the best everything. So no skiving off and no moaning about the hours. That suit you?'

Cate nodded again. 'Can I ask one thing?' she said. 'Who is the boss?'

Wendy and Bill looked at each other and burst out laughing. 'You mean Charlie didn't say?' said Bill, not unkindly.

Cate waited patiently for them to tell her.

'Sorry, mate,' said Bill. 'It's just that normally that's why people want to come and work here. It's great that you're not just a fame junkie looking to hang out with the stars.'

Now Cate really was curious. Wendy was the first to take pity on her.

'British supermodel, pop star, actress, children's book author, animal rights campaigner, rainbow family mother, business woman.' She spoke in a mock chant striking off her fingers as she went. 'Does that help?'

Cate felt her head whirl. Like most of her friends she was a regular reader of celebrity magazines, avidly lapping up the stories of the rich and famous. She knew exactly who Wendy was talking about. This woman was full of energy and talent, as sought after for her acting skills as she was for her ability to champion a charitable cause and get it onto the front pages. She had posed naked to highlight animal cruelty, charmed her way through the war-torn Congo to adopt an abandoned child, set up an organic children's cosmetic line and released the odd number one single for fun. As a result, she had the ear of just about anyone who was anyone. This woman was a legend and she, Cate, was going to be working for her!

'Nancy Kyle.' Cate did her best to keep her cool, but she wanted to jump up and down with excitement.

'That's the one,' said Bill triumphantly. 'My, you're sharp. I can see we're going to have to watch you. Now, if you two ladies don't mind, I've got an engine to check over.'

15

The interview clearly over, Bill turned his back on the two of them.

'Right,' said Wendy. 'Let me show you your cabin.' She marched from the engine room down a little corridor. 'I'm just back there in that cabin and Bill is near the engine, for obvious reasons. Marcus the chef is across from Bill. And here you are,' she said, finally opening a door at the end.

The room was tiny but managed to contain everything Cate could need. There was a bed, a small porthole which looked out onto the waterline and a wardrobe-cum-dressing-table-cum-desk configuration, cleverly designed to take up as little space as possible. There was none of the opulence of the rest of the boat, but there were nods to comfort. A small flat-screen TV had been fitted onto the wall opposite the bunk, over the sink was a shelf holding a kettle and various tea and coffee bags, and there was a fitted hairdryer by a full length mirror.

'OK?' said Wendy. 'Settle yourself in, have a kip, a wash, whatever. If you want to go for a wander around town later, that's fine. Dinner's at eight-thirty if you want it, and tomorrow morning you start your duties.'

Cate collected her suitcase and, returning to her cabin, was suddenly overcome with exhaustion. It was only eleven in the morning but she had been travelling since before dawn. It took Cate a few seconds to clean her teeth and wash her hands and face. Then she checked her phone and fired off a few quick text messages to Monique, her father and Louisa to tell them she had arrived safely and was happily installed on the boat. Naturally she couldn't resist telling them that she was actually working for *the* Nancy Kyle. Then, with the overhead fan wafting cool air onto her bunk, the last thing she did, before she fell asleep, was to carefully lock her cabin door and check that the porthole was firmly closed. As her father was always saying, 'You can't be too careful.'

CHAPTER 2

Cate woke completely refreshed from her deep sleep. The sun was still shining through the porthole and she propped herself up on her elbow to look around at her new home, trying to ignore the small but persistent stabs of homesickness. She had already had a text back from Louisa moaning about the weather, telling her she was so lucky it hurt, and asking her if she had met Nancy yet, which made Cate feel a lot better.

The cabin was painted in white and lemon, which gave it a warm feel, and despite its cell-like proportions – around two metres by four metres – it felt cosy rather than claustrophobic. She swung her feet down to the floor and took a couple of strides over to the kettle, unpacking her rucksack as it boiled. First out was her pride and joy, her pearl white mini laptop, which her father had bought her for her sixteenth birthday, together with decent headphones and a tiny camcorder.

Despite only being fourteen, her brother Arthur was already

a computer genius. He'd installed Skype so that they could talk at any time, had customised the laptop and added some 'Arthur specials'. These included unbreakable internet security and a tracking system, no larger than a two pound coin, that she could keep on the laptop in case it was stolen, or use as a portable device in her bag or even on her mobile. Arthur claimed that, when it was switched on, he could use internet GPS to work out where she was to within a few square metres with just a few clicks. She wasn't quite sure why she needed that, but agreed to it to keep Arthur happy.

It was four-thirty. It would be three-thirty in London now and with a bit of luck Arthur would be online and ready for a chat.

Cate tapped in her security code, plugged in the tiny dongle for internet access and clicked on the communication icon at the bottom of the screen. Suddenly Arthur was there, in his bedroom in West London. His bright bespectacled face lit up her screen, his delight in seeing her evident.

'Sis! How's it going?' His familiar voice was a wonderful sound. The two of them were close, closer than most other brothers and sisters. Throughout their parents' divorce, and in whichever strange country they found themselves, they'd always had each other to laugh or cry with and to depend on. Right now, Cate wanted to reach through the screen and hug him.

'It's great, Arthur, really gorgeous,' said Cate, smiling at her brother instead. 'And you'll never guess what?' She didn't give her brother any time to answer. 'I'm only working for Nancy Kyle! It's Nancy Kyle's yacht!'

'Who? Hang on, I'll Google her,' he said and Cate had to suppress a giggle. For Arthur, the world of fashion and celebrity was a complete no-go zone. 'God – I see who you mean. That Nancy Kyle. Cool. Super-cool. Wait till I tell my mates! Wait till you tell *your* mates!'

'I can't believe it either,' said Cate, 'but, Arthur, the boat is fab – like being in a film. And the navigation computers – well, you'd just be in heaven.'

'What about the crew?' asked Arthur.

'They're OK,' said Cate. 'The captain's an Aussie. He's tough but seems fair and the stewardess, my direct boss, seems really pleased to have someone to help her out. I haven't met the chef yet. How're you all?' asked Cate.

'Honestly,' said Arthur, in mock exasperation, 'we're fine and dandy, just like we were when you left ten hours ago.'

'Yeah, I get the message. I'm missing you, that's all,' said Cate. 'Look, I'm going for a run now. I want to explore the area a bit, get my bearings. I'll call you tomorrow maybe. Oh, and if you bump into Louisa, feel free to tell her about *Catwalk II*. I promise I'll email her properly soon.'

'Sure thing,' said Arthur.

'Thanks. Give my love to Monique and Dad. *Ciao*.'

Arthur planted a sloppy kiss on his screen and Cate laughed and logged off. She packed her laptop carefully back in her bag, and took out her beloved running gear – her cut-offs, a cropped top and her air trainers. There was no better way to get to know a new place than by going jogging, she thought.

Ten minutes later, she was climbing up the spiral staircase to the outer deck. As she passed the middle deck she heard the beat of music playing, and the spicy scent of food cooking. Suddenly starving, she headed for the galley, the obvious source of the smell.

The man inside the immaculate galley had heard her coming, and his head was up, watching her as she knocked on the open door.

'Hi there, you must be Cate,' said a tall man, in a lilting West African accent. 'I'm Marcus the chef, at your service. Welcome aboard.'

His dark face was handsome and open. He was well over six foot tall and, Cate guessed, nearly forty. Beneath his T-shirt, his arms had the bulky muscles of someone who regularly worked out.

'Hi,' said Cate, smiling back at him, glad of a friendly face. 'I start work tomorrow. I was on my way out but I smelt your food and . . .'

'Hungry, eh?' said Marcus, loping across the room in a couple of strides. He reached up to a cupboard set high above the sink and brought out a loaf of French bread and some crackers. Then he produced pâté, soft cheese and cold roast chicken from the fridge and placed them on a thick round wooden board. 'I bet no one's given you a bite to eat since you got here,' he said. He pushed the board towards Cate and handed her a knife and a small jade-green plate which was embossed with a picture of *Catwalk II*.

Cate found herself telling Marcus about her need to have a break from London and to get back to the sunshine and the sea while she ate.

'I guess if anywhere is home then London is and I do love

it,' she explained. 'I do a lot of martial arts and running and that keeps me fit and alert, but I know that, well, there are other places where it isn't such a struggle to stay cheerful – if that makes sense.'

Marcus nodded. 'Sure does,' he said. 'I worked in London for a year once and the traffic damn near drove me crazy. Had fun though.' He smiled fondly at some distant memory. 'You Brits sure know how to throw a good party – and have a good crisis as well.'

Cate wasn't quite sure what he meant by that last remark, but in any case she had finished her food and was itching to get out and explore the town.

'Thanks for that,' she said.

'You're welcome.' Marcus smiled. 'You go out and have fun. Staff dinner is a hot meal in the main salon at eight-thirty and breakfast is a cold, self-service job in the mess room in the basement. In fact, you can eat there any time you like – just help yourself. When Nancy is on board we staff eat in the mess room all the time, but while the cat's away, we dine in style!' Marcus winked at Cate and began carving some meat, deftly slicing it into razor thin slices.

'See you later,' said Cate, and she headed out into the heat of the late Antibes afternoon.

From the circular walkway that ringed the marina she headed towards the old city walls. Suddenly she stopped and turned her entire body towards the sun. It beat down on her face and her bare arms and legs with all the subtlety of a blowtorch, but to Cate, heat starved after a particularly dreary English early summer, it was wonderful.

Cate felt a sudden surge of pure happiness. She was in the South of France, on a boat with people who seemed pretty decent and working for one of the most famous women in the western world. It didn't get much better than this, Cate figured. Talk about striking gold!

She took a little leap over a low wall, put on her Ray-Bans, twisted her hair up under her baseball cap and set off through one of the several archways in the ancient walls that separated the old town from the sea.

Cate walked up the cobbled street, past restaurants crammed with late afternoon diners and turned right onto the main street that ran up from the harbour towards the centre of the town. On either side there were more restaurants, and fish shops, patisseries displaying mouth-watering tarts and cakes, and wine shops with vibrant window displays.

The road climbed upward. She passed a covered market, where the last of the stalls were being cleared away, and started to power-walk up the steep hill until the street began to flatten out. She wanted to follow the coast, so she turned left and headed out onto the promontory that stuck out into the crystal blue Mediterranean.

The road that wound around the point was crowded with tourists and cars, with mopeds weaving their way in and out of the traffic. To the right, honey-coloured houses rose precariously upward, clinging tightly to the hillsides. To her left, a frighteningly low wall seemed to be the only thing protecting motorists and walkers from plunging fifty metres to the rocks and sea below.

Cate began to run downhill. The road quietened as it

curved back off from the point, still following the coast but passing through the residential area of the Cap d'Antibes, a place Cate had read about so often in celebrity magazines. This was the land of the rich and famous, film and pop stars and Russian oligarchs, where large chateaux and tastefully exclusive low-rise apartment blocks nestled amongst greenery and manicured lawns.

Cate came to a beach and ran onto it with delight. At the edge of the golden sand was a sailing club – a clapperboard, wind-bleached building. The masts of dinghies, marooned on the sand, clanked and banged in the breeze. Beside them a group of teenagers had rigged up a volleyball net and were effortlessly batting a ball back and forth over the net.

Cate stood and watched them for a few minutes, suddenly missing her friends back home. One of the boys – tall with dark hair and blue eyes – noticed her and smiled. Cate smiled back uncertainly. He gestured with the ball – would she like to join in? When Cate shook her head shyly, he pulled a rueful face and carried on with the game.

Perhaps another day, thought Cate. She started off again, jogging past the club and then sprinting along the sandy beach until it ran out. Catching her breath, she turned right and began to climb up again, into the maze of little alleyways that criss-crossed the peninsula.

Pine trees towered above, releasing their sweet oily smell in the late afternoon heat. The noise and life of the beach faded behind her. A few birds flew lazily about and a cat slunk in and out of fenced-off gardens. Away from the sea breeze the temperature was even more intense. Cate ran carefully, mindful of the jagged edges of the pavements. She had no real idea where she was going, but she had her little compass and she was on the narrow part of a peninsula. She couldn't get very lost.

Cate marvelled as she got closer to the huge mansions which loomed at the end of high-gated drives. There were warning signs everywhere – in French, English and Russian – telling passersby to beware of the dogs or electric fences or patrolling guards. Yet most of the houses were clearly shut up and the streets deserted.

Suddenly, two hundred metres ahead of her, a man appeared, crossing the road from one small alleyway to another. He was the same height and build as Marcus, and was wearing the same bright blue T-shirt. Although his dark face was partially obscured, the resemblance was so uncanny that, for a few seconds, Cate was convinced it was the friendly chef. She nearly called out to him but he vanished and, by the time she reached the crossroads and looked down the alleyway, it was empty. She walked along it for a few metres and poked her nose over the first gate she came to, then the second. She even checked down an overgrown path which ran alongside another house, before realising how ridiculous she was being – Marcus was on the boat getting supper ready.

She was still laughing at herself when she heard a noise that froze her to the spot. It was a rasping sound, with a low keening. It was the sound of pain and fear and it was coming nearer and nearer.

Instinctively, Cate pushed herself back into the side alley and stood completely still. As she stared back up to the top of the alleyway, a fair-haired man crawled into her line of vision. His face was battered and bloody, one leg stretched out uselessly behind him. It was obvious that any movement took a huge effort and the gasping Cate could hear was a sign that he was not going to be able to carry on for much longer.

He finally gave up the struggle and collapsed onto the ground. As he did so, he turned his head towards Cate. For a few agonised seconds they made eye contact. Then his eyes closed and the colour drained from his already pale face.

Cate was about to rush to his assistance when suddenly she heard a clatter of footsteps coming up the hill. Two men, wearing black T-shirts and jeans, rushed to either side of the injured man and, to Cate's horror, turned him over onto his back and began to kick his body and legs.

Once, in Kosovo with her father, she had witnessed a teenage boy being beaten by a gang of villagers who had accused him of theft. It had been horrible to see – the boy whimpering and cowed, trying hopelessly to protect his bloodied face as the blows rained in. Cate had desperately wanted to help, even tried to get to him through the crowd, but her dad had held her back and eventually a group of Danish peacekeepers had waded into the fray and rescued the terrified boy. Later, her father had read her the riot act about interfering in dangerous situations and she knew he was right, but for months afterwards she had felt guilty that she hadn't helped.

This time there were no friendly peacekeepers around the corner. And by the time Cate got help this man would be dead. In desperation she looked around for a weapon. The wall behind her was topped with a short metal fence held upright with wooden bars. Frantically she groped at the first bar but it wouldn't budge. The second one, too, was fixed solid. Cate looked around and to her relief spotted some older and less well-maintained railings further down the alley. She crept carefully to the first of the posts, took a deep breath and tugged hard. It came away in her hands immediately. It felt heavy and solid, like a police baton.

She was terrified that the movement she had made would alert the two thugs, but it seemed that they were enjoying their work too much to notice anything else.

It was now or never. Cate took a deep breath and ran towards the nearest man, who had his back to her, his long lank hair falling over his T-shirt. As she had done so many times before in her kickboxing classes, she launched herself into midair and landed with both her feet on his lower back. Mid-kick, he was totally off balance and fell forward, sprawling over his victim. The other man paused, frozen by the shock of her arrival, but he recovered quickly and within a few seconds was putting out a huge hand to grab the bar that Cate was wielding. She whirled around just out of his reach, using the momentum from her turn to strike his still-sprawling comrade on the side of his forehead. Just about to stand up, he fell back down again, clutching his head.

Sensing a blow coming in, Cate turned back to the second man, ducking as she did so. She felt his arm move centimetres above her head, but before he could take another punch at her, she twisted around and kicked backwards, viciously, into his groin. As he doubled over, she whirled back to face him and brought the bar down hard onto his exposed neck. He staggered, groaning in pain and shock, then, seeing Cate bearing down on him again, he turned and fled down the dusty road.

His colleague was now on his feet and reaching into his pocket. Cate saw the glint of metal and, a split second later, she kicked at it with her right leg. She felt contact, and the gun flew through the air, disappearing into bushes twenty metres away. Now he too had had enough and ran, still holding his head, after the other man.

The whole episode had taken less than two minutes. Shocked at herself and the entire turn of events, Cate turned back to the man she had rescued. He was sitting up, staring at Cate in amazement.

'Who are you?' He spoke in French, but with a thick accent from somewhere else. 'Just who the hell are you?'

Cate stayed silent. She knelt down and leant her left shoulder towards him. He slung his right arm around her neck and somehow managed to stand up and put his weight onto his good leg as they staggered out of the alley.

'They could be back any minute,' Cate said to him in French. 'I'm going to hide you and then get help.'

The man nodded towards a side road. 'Down there is a good place to hide. Then you must get away. I will be OK.'

They made their way slowly and painfully past several houses until the man finally gestured for her to stop outside a black metal gate. Breathing hard and struggling for air, he used his free hand to push against the gate and it opened slowly onto a gravel drive. Together, the two of them managed to half stagger, half crawl a few metres up the overgrown drive before it became clear that the man would get no further. Looking about her for somewhere safe to hide him, Cate gently manoeuvred him as far as she could into the mesh of branches which overhung the edge of a large lawn.

His eyes closed and his face drawn, the man sank gratefully onto the grass. 'Can you hear me?' said Cate in French. Shaking with shock, she remembered his accent. '*Ti menia slishish?*'

The sound of his native tongue brought the man round from his stupor and he spoke back to her in Russian. 'You're one hell of a girl,' he said, attempting a grin. 'Now listen. Tell the Roman that Andrei – that's me – says he has to look for the good times. They're all there, everything the Roman was looking for. Everything . . .'

'I don't know what you mean. Who is the Roman?' Russian was never Cate's best language, and she began to wonder if she was worse at it than she had thought, or if the man was delirious. Andrei was clearly in a bad way. He had gone the colour of pale chalk and was pouring sweat. Cate opened his jacket to see if there was any blood loss but couldn't find any obvious wounds.

She made up her mind. 'I'm going to get help. Stay here and I'll be back. Stay here.' Without waiting for an answer, she got to her feet and ran back down the drive. As she reached the gate she turned to look. The man was completely hidden by the trees. He would be safe there. For now, at least.

CHAPTER 3

After checking that the alleyway was empty, Cate headed back up to the scene of the fight. She stopped to pick up her rucksack and, after a brief hesitation, ran over to where the gun had landed.

She kicked and scuffed at the bushes with her trainer and felt her foot connect with something hard. She bent down and picked up a smallish pistol, a Beretta, the type she had seen carried by bodyguards all over the world. She thought about leaving it there in the hope that someone else would find it and hand it to the police, but the men would probably come back to look for it and she didn't want them using it against anyone else. Worse still – Cate shuddered at the thought – a kid might find it and hurt themselves or others.

Cate hated guns and what they could do, although she knew very well how to use one. Every time she visited her mother in LA, her mother had insisted that Cate took gun lessons for her own defence, and so she learnt, in spite of herself, how to load and reload a gun in seconds, becoming skilled at shooting moving targets and distinguishing between different pistols and guns.

Cate unloaded the gun and put the safety catch on. She dropped the six bullets into a side pocket of the rucksack and tucked the gun right at the bottom before heading back towards the main road.

The adrenalin from the fight had long since worn off and as she ran she suddenly felt very vulnerable, and terrified that the two thugs would reappear. She felt as if thousands of hostile eyes were watching from the shuttered windows, and it didn't help that the bright sun was being replaced with the dull light of early evening. As she reached the coast road, it was with utter relief that she spotted a police vehicle parked a few metres ahead of her.

Cate ran over to the car and banged frantically on the window, speaking in English in her panic, before realising her mistake and switching to French.

'There's been a fight – a man attacked just up there,' she panted. 'He is in a bad way and he needs help . . .'

She trailed off, suddenly conscious that the two *gendarmes*, who were sitting inside the car sipping coffee, were not looking that impressed.

'OK, were they French, English, what?' said the younger man, leaning out of the window to stare at Cate.

'Russian, I think. Well, the man who was attacked is definitely Russian.'

The *gendarme* sat back in his seat and exchanged glances

with his partner, an older, fatter man with slicked back hair.

Cate was enraged by their lack of urgency. 'He is very badly hurt. He needs an ambulance.'

'OK, OK.' The older one sounded bored but he put his coffee slowly into the holder. 'We'll take a look. Hop in and show us the way.'

Cate scrambled into the rear of the police car. It smelt of stale sweat and strong coffee. Sandwiches and sweet wrappers were scattered liberally on the floor.

'Just up there.' She pointed into the maze of small roads.

With a dramatic sigh, the second *gendarme* gunned the engine, wrenched the steering wheel, U-turned across the path of oncoming traffic and headed up into the hills. After a few seconds he spoke. 'OK, young lady, what exactly did you see?'

'I was out running,' Cate said. 'I saw a man crawling along, he was injured. And then two other men came and well – attacked him like they wanted to kill him.'

'Then what happened?'

Cate opened her mouth to tell them that she had fought off two grown men and then realised she would sound like a complete fantasist.

She thought fast.

'Well, I screamed at them and they ran away,' she said lamely, aware of how unlikely this sounded. 'And then I helped the man into a garden and hid him . . .' Her voice trailed off. The silence that followed spoke volumes.

Cate spotted a familiar side road. 'Turn up here,' she said. The car lurched and bounced up the track, took another turning and suddenly they were back at the scene of the fight.

Cate gestured to the gateway of the house where she had left Andrei.

'He's in there,' she said in a pleading voice. 'He's in a bad way.'

'OK. We'll go and take a look,' said the younger *gendarme*. 'But you'd better not be wasting our time,' he added sternly.

The three of them got out of the car and stood for a few seconds looking down the gloomy, overgrown driveway. The sun was dropping down over the houses now, the air felt cooler and Cate could hear the first rasping calls of the cicadas. She was very glad of the two men standing beside her, methodically checking their guns.

Cate walked towards the gate and pushed it open, the two men following behind her.

Even before she reached the clump of trees, Cate sensed rather than saw that the injured man was gone. She went through the motions of pushing through the undergrowth, walked around the edges of vast lawn and she even borrowed a torch from one of the policemen to shine into the darkest areas of bushes – but there was nothing and no one there.

'He must have crawled away,' said Cate lamely. 'He was definitely here.'

She pointed at the flattened grass. The younger *gendarme* crouched down and silently stared at the spot. Then he stood up slowly.

'Let's go,' he said flatly. The three of them walked back to the car, the *gendarmes* on either side of Cate like a pair of bodyguards.

Cate climbed wearily into the car and waited for the lecture.

She was surprised then, when the older policeman began to talk quietly to her.

'Look – what's your name?' He went on without waiting for an answer. 'You're new around here, right?'

Cate nodded.

'Now listen closely, young lady. This place is changing fast. Criminals are coming in from Eastern Europe, Asia, South America faster than we can count them. Our local criminals used to play by some sort of basic rules. But not these new guys.' He shook his head theatrically. 'They carry guns, use tear gas, trade women, children, drugs, medicines – whatever makes the most money at the time. They fight their customers, they fight with cops, but most of all they fight each other. They will beat the hell out of their best friend if they have to. You might have seen a fight or you might be lying. I can't see any real reason why you would make up something like this so I'm inclined to believe you. But either way it doesn't matter. If we wasted our time on every punch up between guys with funny names from remote countries, well, we would be drowning in paperwork and we wouldn't do anything else. You get it?'

Cate got it. But she remembered the injured man's fear, the terror in his eyes and she knew she had to try one more time.

'But what if they find him again? He needs our help,' she said.

Without even turning round to look at Cate, the younger man spoke. 'If we did look for him all night, call out dogs and helicopters and if we did find him – do you know what he'd say? He'd say he'd had an accident and fallen over and that he had never seen you before in his life. So forget what you saw. It's not your problem. Where do you want us to drop you?'

No doubt he was right. It was the equivalent of her father's advice that day back in Kosovo. 'Think before you rush in, Cate. You can't save the world – no one can.'

Suddenly exhausted, she couldn't face making her own way back to the boat. 'Could you take me to the marina, please?' she asked in a small voice. 'I'm staying on a boat there.'

'Not owned by a Russian, I hope.' The younger *gendarme* spluttered with laughter. 'OK, we'll drop you there.'

The police car pulled to a halt in the large car park by the marina.

'Er, thanks.' Cate didn't know what else to say.

'OK – take care now,' said the younger one.

'Watch out for the bad guys,' said the older one.

Cate didn't wait to watch them drive off. She headed into the marina and reached *Catwalk II*, bobbing calmly at her moorings. She looked at her watch – ten past eight. She had only been gone for a few hours but so much had happened in that time it felt more like days. As she dragged herself up the walkway, the waft of delicious smells coming from the galley made her realise that she was truly famished.

Marcus must have heard her coming. He poked his head around the corner of the galley and called to her. 'Twenty minutes to dinner, Cate. Don't be late.'

Cate took a deep breath and tried to sound casual. 'Marcus, were you out this afternoon?' She felt slightly foolish even asking.

Marcus gave her a questioning look. 'No, man,' he said.

35

'Been on the boat most of the day cooking, getting the galley stocked up and listening to music. Why do you ask?'

Cate shook her head. 'Sorry,' she said. 'I just thought I saw you up by the Cap earlier. I was running there.'

'Nope,' he said. 'Must have been my double.'

That's that then, thought Cate. She headed back to the staff quarters, sinking gratefully down onto the bed in her little cabin. Although she was exhausted, her mind was racing. The boy with the volleyball, the fight, the desperate man, the gun. Suddenly she sat up in horror, her stomach churning with the dreadful realisation.

The gun! She still had the gun! How could she have forgotten? She should have told the police about it when they were doubting her. She could hand it in now of course, but after the dismissive way the *gendarmes* had treated her, she didn't much feel like going back to them any time soon. As Cate groaned at her own stupidity, there was a rap on the door and Wendy appeared.

'Cate, dinner's served upstairs in the salon in ten minutes.'

Cate heaved herself off the bed, showered quickly and then pulled on her linen trousers and a T-shirt. She would have to think about the gun later.

Upstairs, the solid mahogany table was set with the jade-green china and crystal glasses. Someone had lit candles and the wall chandeliers glimmered and sparkled reflective light over the highly polished wood and brass.

Wendy grinned when she saw Cate's stunned face. 'Don't get used to it,' she laughed. 'It's kind of a special occasion. Bill just passed his final nautical exams, I got a call from my waster

36

of a boyfriend at last and we all thought it would be a nice way to welcome you onboard.'

'Sit down,' said Bill, pointing to a chair opposite Cate and pouring her some sparkling white grape juice that fizzed in the crystal flute. Cleaned up from their earlier meeting he now looked younger and more approachable. No more than thirty, Cate decided.

He and Wendy seemed like such decent people that she was tempted to confide in them. But then she remembered Bill's words – that he didn't want any trouble.

They'd never believe her anyway, they'd just think she was a drama queen, or a nutter and that would be her card marked for good. She wasn't ready to go home yet.

No, in the circumstances it was definitely best to keep quiet and so, as Bill proposed a toast, Cate made a big effort to smile.

'To *Catwalk II* and all who sail on her,' he said. 'And where is that Marcus when you need him?'

'I'm here, man, don't rush me.' Marcus was carrying a large casserole. He placed it on a mat on the white linen tablecloth and proceeded to ladle out generous portions of steak in a rich red sauce topped with crispy brown miniature dumplings.

He smiled. 'Tuck in, guys.'

Cate ate heartily, feeling more human with every mouthful. Suddenly the events of the day seemed like a dream, as if they had happened to someone else. She found herself relaxing and telling Wendy about how she knew Charlie (he was an old school friend of her dad's) and about her mad mum in LA who only rang when she was feeling low and then got upset if Cate ever asked anything remotely mother-like of her.

In return, Wendy confided that her American boyfriend was a loser but far too gorgeous to give up on, no matter how many times he forgot to ring.

Marcus, who was sitting opposite Cate, seemed very quiet compared to his earlier chattiness. 'I forgot to ask, how was your run?' he said finally, his words wrenching Cate back to the chaos of the last few hours.

She looked up at him warily, but his face was expressionless. 'It was, er, well, OK,' she said lamely. 'Nice views.'

'Did you see the Russians?'

This time she stared at him blankly, a feeling of panic rising from her stomach.

'The beautiful people who hang out on the beach. They're mostly Russians.' He grinned. Cate felt herself relax. 'It's all Russians here now, you know – in fact, you might be better off forgetting about French and learning to speak Russian.'

'She does already,' Bill suddenly chimed in. 'She's quite the linguist,' he continued with a friendly wink at Cate. 'That's why I took her on. Thought she might be useful when Nancy brings her international friends onboard.'

'You clearly have hidden depths,' Marcus said slowly, his dark eyes giving nothing away. 'Anything else we should know?'

He was still smiling but an anxious voice in Cate's head was starting to chatter. Was this just easy banter or was there more of a sinister undertone to Marcus's questions? Cate knew that she was way too tired to make a rational judgement.

She shook her head and looked at her watch. 'Do you mind if I skip pudding? I think it's time that I turned in. It's been a long day.'

'I'm not surprised.' Marcus sat his large frame back in his chair. 'I can see you're going to be good for our health as well as our intellect, Cate Carlisle – I'm exhausted, too. I won't be long behind you.'

Back in her cabin, Cate lay in her bunk and sent the promised email to Louisa. She kept it light, telling her about the yacht and the good-looking guys in the sailing club. The other stuff could wait and, in any case, Cate thought that Louisa would accuse her of suffering from sunstroke if she told her about Andrei.

The gentle motion of the water just a few metres below her bunk rocked her as if she were in a hammock and through her tiny porthole she could see the moonlight glinting on the water. Cate closed her eyes and breathed deeply, waiting for sleep to come.

Half an hour later she was still, annoyingly, very much awake. She had heard both the men and Wendy turn in to their cabins and the sound of several groups of happy people wandering back to their boats from an evening out. She had tried absolutely everything she could think of to get herself to sleep but instead, by midnight, she had rather crossly come to the conclusion that there was nothing for it but to heed her dad's advice – if you can't sleep, don't stay in bed.

With a sigh Cate stepped out of her bunk, pulled on a sweatshirt, shorts and her deck shoes and unlocked her cabin door. She tiptoed quietly to the spiral staircase and up onto the middle deck. She paused by the main glass doors, trying to remember the six figure security code that Wendy had given to her earlier that day. Cate typed in the number, pulled at the handle and heard a subdued click as the doors glided open. She stepped out into the warm night air.

Around her, the dimmed lights of the boats hardly detracted from the brilliant starlight and the almost full moon. A few hundred metres away, the walls of the town looked black and imposing.

She sat quietly on one of the deck cushions, enjoying the feeling of being the only one awake in the world, when she heard low male voices coming from along the pontoon. Although she couldn't hear what they were saying, the pace of the conversation sounded urgent and anxious.

Cate knew that it was almost impossible to gauge the distance of sound on water, but still she craned her neck around the side of the deck to see if she could spot the owners of the voices. At the far end of the pontoon, as it curved away from her line of vision, she could just make out the shape of two men standing close together. Their body language was tense. A blond man with his back to her was frantically waving his hands around and the other was rubbing his forehead.

As Cate's eyes became more accustomed to the gloom, she saw that the large man facing her was none other than Marcus – who had just made a big show of going to bed early.

Or his double again, she thought grimly. She paused for a moment. The last time she had thought she'd seen Marcus away from the boat, a man had been nearly beaten to death. This time she intended to find out, for certain, if it was Marcus, and what he was talking about.

Cate looked around, gauging the best way to get nearer to the men without them noticing her. The walkway between

Catwalk II and the pontoon was still down although the little gate at the end of it was locked with a number coded device. She hopped quietly over the top of it and moved quickly to shelter under the awning of the boat opposite.

She tried to think rationally. The men were talking out in the open so they clearly weren't expecting eavesdroppers. If she just kept quiet and moved along, using the boats for cover, she could get close to them. She glanced along the pontoon, selecting her route before she started out.

Cate passed the first three boats without incident and paused in the darkness for a few seconds to check that the men were still talking. The next four boats were lit up by the moon so Cate crossed back over the pontoon into the shadows.

She picked her next destination and made a dash for it, coming to rest in between the prow of two boats. Terrified that Marcus may have seen the movement, she paused and listened, but the murmur of conversation continued.

Only a few more boats to go and then surely she would get a clear view of the men. She steeled herself to make the last few dashes, and four boats later she was only a few metres away from her target. By now, the murmurs had become clear words and she listened intently, her heart pounding hard. The men were in darkness, the boats around them locked up and silent. They were speaking in Russian but Cate could clearly pick out words. Missing . . . man-hunt . . . inside information . . . smuggling.

She was only half shocked, then, to see the glint of metal tucked into the back of the blond-haired man's trousers and a wire which was clearly some sort of receiver running from the back pocket to his left ear. This was scary stuff and Cate suddenly began to wish she had never given into her natural curiosity. She felt frightened and cross with herself and she began to plan her route back to the boat and safety.

Then Cate heard Marcus mention the name Andrei – he had to be talking about the man she had helped earlier that day. Just a few seconds later, his colleague put a hand up to his ear and gave a visible start.

'There's a new mobile phone signal right here,' he said urgently to Marcus. 'The signal is less than three metres away. Who's there?' he called out.

Immediately the two men dived sideways, their hands drawing their guns as they went. In the silence, Cate fought a rising wave of panic as she tried to work out what to do. Should she stay quiet and hope that they didn't find her? She pulled her phone out of her pocket and her trembling fingers pressed the off button firmly, realising as she did, that it was way too late for that.

The two men were unnervingly still, but Cate knew it was just a question of time before they started their search. If she stayed where she was they would find her in seconds. She looked frantically around her for an escape route.

They would see her immediately if she tried to board a boat. There was only one option – the water. Without thinking, she slipped off her deck shoes, pushed her phone back into its waterproof holder, tucked it into her pocket and edged backwards as quietly as she could. Her feet dangled over the edge of the pontoon and she bit her lip, bracing herself for contact with the inky liquid below. It felt surprisingly warm.

Making as few ripples as possible, she slid silently into the sea, gripping tightly onto the edge of the pontoon with her fingertips for a few seconds longer whilst she waited for the unpleasant sensation of her clothes absorbing the water. Then she let go and began to swim silently alongside the boats and out into the centre of the marina.

By now, the two men had edged back out of the shadows and, with their guns drawn, were checking out the pontoon. Cate watched in horror as Marcus moved cautiously towards the spot where she had been crouching just a few seconds before. He stood there, his gaze sweeping from left to right across the water. Suddenly he spoke in a voice that was quiet but menacing. 'Cate Carlisle, I know you're out there. Get out and let's talk or I'll get really annoyed.'

The water suddenly felt like an icy shroud around her body. How on earth did Marcus know it was her? She looked up at the huge hull of the boat above her – there was no way up its shiny sides. She was a strong swimmer but her speed would be no match for the bullets.

Marcus spoke again. 'Cate, you're not quite as smart as you think you are. You left your shoes behind. You've got ten seconds to get out.'

'I'll scream!' Cate spoke with a vehemence that surprised her. 'I'll scream and wake the whole marina up.'

Through the darkness she heard Marcus's reply. 'Well, you can try, but then my friend just behind you will shove your head under the water so quickly that you'll wish you'd kept your mouth shut.'

Horrified, Cate turned and saw the grinning head of

Marcus's blond-haired partner silently treading water a metre behind her. He reached out a hand and grabbed the scruff of her T-shirt, twisting it tightly so that no matter how she tried to pull away, she was helpless as the large man towed her slowly back to the pontoon and to a grim-faced Marcus.

Marcus held her by the shoulders, dragged her unceremoniously out of the water and dumped her on the pontoon. She stared up at him, her look of defiance rapidly turning to fear as he pushed the barrel of the gun in her chest and simultaneously raised his index finger to his lips. She debated whether or not to try to fight him off, but her clothes were wet and heavy and the element of surprise that had stood her in such good stead earlier in the day was gone. She was totally helpless and very, very scared.

CHAPTER 4

Marcus began to laugh. 'Cate, what are you playing at?' he said. 'Aren't you meant to be fast asleep in your cabin?'

Stunned, Cate said nothing.

He spoke again, more gently. 'Cate, you're not in danger. I promise you.'

Cate tried desperately to read his expression. Was this some sort of trap?

'OK,' sighed Marcus. 'I can see I'm going to have trouble convincing you I'm not about to finish you off with a bullet or drown you in the marina. Kids today . . .' he shook his head theatrically, '. . . they're so damn cynical. Don't worry, Piot, I'll deal with this.'

He grabbed her hands and heaved her to her feet. 'Come on,' he said briskly, quick-marching her back towards *Catwalk II*. 'We'll get you warmed up and then we are going to talk.'

Ten minutes later, Cate was sitting in the tiny galley

wrapped in a huge towel, drinking a cup of hot chocolate. Marcus was perched across the narrow bar from her, his dark eyes staring directly into hers.

'Right, Cate. Tell me why on earth you crept up on us like that? What were you thinking?'

Cate was silent for a few seconds, whilst she gathered her thoughts. Marcus waited patiently.

'I saw you this afternoon, up on the Cap,' she said quietly.

'Yes, you did,' agreed Marcus. 'I'm sorry I lied. I was meeting a – a business contact but he didn't turn up. It was kind of private, that's why I didn't want to talk about it.'

'Your meeting wasn't with someone called Andrei?' Cate asked, watching closely for his reaction.

'How in God's name do you know that?' he asked her curtly, his eyes wide. 'Have you seen him?'

Cate weighed up his response. If he was telling the truth, then it explained why Andrei was alone and helpless when he was attacked. If he was lying – well, that could mean a hundred different things.

'Cate, this is important,' Marcus said urgently. 'Andrei's missing, he could be in real danger. We need to find him fast, for all sorts of reasons.'

Could she trust Marcus? She remembered her feeling of ease around him when they first met, then the fear as he ruthlessly stuck a gun at her chest. She looked at his anxious face and made up her mind. She told him everything: about her run, the fight, the aftermath and her encounter with the *gendarmes*. Marcus let her talk, his face expressionless and then, when she had finally finished, he reached for his phone, punched in a number and spoke quickly into the receiver.

'Piot, we have a lead on Andrei. I'll meet you by the car in five.'

He rang off. 'I just can't believe I was so close to Andrei – I could have helped him,' he said regretfully. He paused for a few seconds, then spoke again. 'Right, can you do your best to tell me exactly where you left Andrei? And then, Cate, you are going to bed.'

Cate opened her mouth to protest but Marcus silenced her. 'You've done enough and you look half dead. We'll take over now and I'll explain everything in the morning. Trust me.'

He was right about the exhaustion. Cate felt cold and tired and despite her best efforts her eyelids were drooping. It was the second time that she'd had to guide someone to the place of the attack and wearily she sketched a map which picked out the yacht club, the turnings and finally the large villa where she had last seen Andrei. As he studied the map Marcus nodded his head.

'I know where that is,' he said grimly. 'There's a safe house nearby. He must be holed up there. I just hope we won't be too late. Cate, you've done well.'

Cate had just enough energy left to drag herself down the stairs to her cabin. As she collapsed onto her bunk she heard Marcus's footsteps moving quietly back along the pontoon outside her window. She tried to work out whether she had done the right thing by confiding in him but she was too tired to think any more. Seconds later she was asleep.

Cate woke with a start to the unmistakable sound of a

helicopter clattering overhead. The vibrations from the propellers were so strong that for a few surreal seconds she thought the chopper was going to land on the boat itself. Then she heard screaming and laughter coming from outside and, pulling on shorts and a T-shirt, raced up onto the outer deck.

An extraordinary sight greeted her. A bright pink helicopter hovered metres above the boat, hardly clearing mast height. The passenger side of the chopper was open and out of it was leaning one of the most famous women in the world. Her trademark, razored red bob – one of the most copied haircuts of the moment – clashed horribly with the pink paintwork of the helicopter and an enormous pair of sunglasses covered most of her fine-boned face. Her wide, thick-lipped mouth was painted with lipstick which perfectly matched her hair colour and her voice, incredibly, rose above the noise of the machine.

'*Catwalk II* – I love you, you are so beeeeuuutiful, I love you! Bill, love ya, Wends, love ya, whoever you are in the cute shorts, love ya. See you in a mo, guys, so get yourselves together pronto, no pressure. Love ya.'

The raucous voice, with its strong Essex accent, and the clatter of the helicopter brought people out onto the decks of nearby boats to stare in amazement. Then the helicopter rose up into the air, turned abruptly to the right and was gone. Nancy Kyle was in town!

It was only just after nine, but as Cate went back down below she found Wendy already hard at work in the master cabin.

'Good, you're here,' the South African said calmly. 'I hope

you enjoyed your lie-in. Now it's time to earn your keep.'

For the next thirty minutes, Cate, conscious that this was the first chance to prove herself, worked harder than she had ever done in her life. The beds were turned down and aired, already clean bathrooms were made fresh and sparkling, any trace of human activity was removed from the thick pile carpets in the lounge and bedrooms and mahogany furniture and brass fittings were polished.

Finally, just as Cate was straightening the last of the thick, fluffy towels on the top deck, the opening act of the Nancy Kyle show began.

First into view on the pontoon came a man and a woman, so strikingly different from each other that they could almost have been picked for the visual effect they created as they walked side by side. The man was very tall and painfully thin, with black spiky hair adding to his height. His dark, Asian features, all razor-sharp cheek bones and pointed nose, contrasted almost shockingly with the round blondness of the petite woman at his side. Even her painfully high heels, ridiculously unsuitable for the slotted marina walkway, didn't bring her up to the chest of her companion and she had to trot to keep up with him. In turn, he flounced rather than walked, looking, Cate thought, sulky and displeased at life in general.

'Lulu and Jules,' said Wendy, who was, by now, standing on the outer deck ready to greet them. 'One is Nancy's ever loyal and incredibly efficient PA, the other her stylist, fitness guru and personal astrologer. I'll leave you to guess which one is which.'

'Jules, Lulu, welcome aboard,' she said cheerfully as the

couple reached the gangplank. 'It's great to see you both again. Help yourself to deck shoes.'

With evident relief, Lulu kicked off her heels and walked up the gangplank. 'Good to see you too, Wendy,' she said in an accent that Cate struggled to place. Czech? Hungarian, maybe? 'Sorry about the surprise, but well, you know how Nancy is. She only decided to come here when she woke up this morning.'

Wendy shrugged and smiled. Lulu, completely ignoring Cate's outstretched hand, walked onto the deck and flopped down on one of the cream sofas.

Meanwhile, Jules was wrestling with the straps of a soft leather rucksack. 'I am simply not wearing other peoples' deck shoes,' he shouted crossly up the gangplank. 'It is too, too gross for words. I have brought my own.'

Cate felt the urge to giggle, before catching a warning glance from Wendy.

'Cate, can you go and help Jules with his bags?' she said quietly. 'Lulu, you must be desperate for a cold drink.'

Five minutes later the two newcomers – Jules resplendent in a pair of highly polished snakeskin deck shoes – were settled on the inner deck, sipping cold lemonade from tall, frosted glasses.

'This is Cate,' said Wendy.

Jules looked her slowly up and down. 'English,' he said, making the word sound remarkably like an insult. At any second Cate expected him to shudder and cover his eyes.

'Cate is my right-hand girl,' said Wendy firmly, ignoring Jules's rudeness. 'If I'm not around, just ask her for anything you need. She is multilingual.'

'Take it back. Can't be English, then,' murmured Jules.

'If Wendy thinks you're OK, then you must be,' Lulu said grudgingly. 'But a word of warning, my dear. Don't get above your station. And you may be a pretty young thing but don't even think about flirting with Nancy's boyfriends. She really, really, hates it when servants do that.'

Jules nodded gravely. There was silence. Cate looked at Wendy, who gave her the smallest of winks.

'So no kids today, Lulu?' Wendy asked, changing the subject tactfully.

'They probably don't even know Nancy's gone yet,' said Lulu, shaking her head and glancing at her large diamanté watch. 'I expect the nanny will tell them sometime today. Nancy says she needs a break from the demands of motherhood. She says she is exhausted and badly in need of some "me" time.'

As if on cue, Cate became aware of a furore just along the walkway. She turned to look and saw two young men each pulling three large leather suitcases, followed by the unmistakable figure of Nancy Kyle. She looked magnificent, striding along with the grace of one who had spent years on catwalks and in front of cameras. She was a dazzle of primary colours – her short red hair glinted like a helmet, her canary yellow, skin-tight top barely reached down to the sky-blue pencil skirt which clung lovingly to every curve of her shapely bottom and willowy thighs.

Wow, thought Cate as she stared helplessly at Nancy.

'Wow,' whispered Bill who together with Marcus had come out to greet their boss.

'Ahoy there, beautiful people. I'm back.'

Bill, Wendy and Marcus all made a rush for the gangway. Bill got there first and offered Nancy his hand, Wendy got a kiss and Marcus definitely an admiring glance. Cate was entranced by the whole spectacle, but in the general mêlée Marcus grabbed her by the elbow and suddenly the racket faded into the background.

'You and I need to talk,' he said ominously. And with that he was gone, leaving Cate feeling deflated and anxious.

An hour later, as the heat climbed to its midday high, Nancy summoned her entire staff to the top deck. Lying flat on her back on a teak sun lounger, her long legs covered in sun cream and her pale face protected by a parasol, she waved for them to sit down.

'Hi, guys,' said Nancy quietly, keeping her eyes firmly closed. 'I want a really chilled time in the next week or so, OK? No visitors, no fans and definitely no horrible paparazzi. It's been catwalk, catwalk, magazine covers, interviews, aeroplanes, kids, God knows what since January and I'm bloody shattered. All I want is sleep, sunshine, good nosh, peace and quiet. Got it?'

Everyone nodded vehemently. A bit of a waste of time, thought Cate, as Nancy still hadn't bothered to open her eyes. Suddenly the strains of a mobile phone rang out harshly, cutting through the hot silence like a bullet. Nancy grabbed her diamond-encrusted BlackBerry and sat bolt up right.

'Darling,' she said loudly, valiantly trying to tone down her Essex accent. 'Darling, why didn't you tell me you were at the

Roc? How fabulous, I'd love to. Tonight? You know me, always ready to party – especially with you lovely, lively Irish lads. See you tonight, darling – later!'

She lay back down again. 'The Irish Saint,' she said, by way of explanation. 'Can someone book me a car for ten tonight? And Marcus, I'm hungry; I want some chips. Those fat ones not the thin ones. Proper British chips. No salt. Tomato ketchup – Heinz, no French muck. And still water. I don't want to bloat.'

'On its way,' said Marcus cheerfully, heading off towards the stairway. 'By the way, can I borrow Cate for an hour or so later, Wendy?' he said as he passed her. 'Just need help with some shopping and forward planning.'

'Yeah, OK,' said Wendy. 'But she has to unpack Nancy's clothes first, all right?'

'Perfect,' said Marcus, without even looking in Cate's direction.

Cate was soon standing in the vast walk-in wardrobe of the master bedroom suite. Six suitcases worth of clothes had been laid out on the bed and she was surrounded by a chaotic mass of tissue paper and other packing paraphernalia, but for all that, she felt as if she had died and gone to heaven.

Dresses from every designer in every hue lay on the vast bed. There was a midnight blue Roland Mouret cocktail dress and a flamboyant Roberto Cavalli evening number. Nestling underneath them, Cate spotted a tiny scrap of a Dolce and Gabbana skirt in asymmetrical orange and lemon and next to that lay a Jill Birkin multi-coloured kaftan and a vivid pink Versace shift dress.

She counted twenty Jil Sander T-shirts in an entire spectrum of colours, four swimsuits and eight bikinis, ranging from teeny bits of string to Fifties-styled short briefs. There were Hermès scarves and Mulberry beach bags. And then there were the shoes! Cate took them pair by pair and laid them reverentially on the floor.

Impossibly tall Jimmy Choos competed with red-soled Louboutins for attention, whilst several pairs of strappy peep-toes by Manolo Blahnik mingled with gorgeously frivolous flip flops from Miu Miu. Cate had a brief flashback of trying on eight pound flip flops in Accessorize with Louisa and felt slightly hysterical. So much for just one person. Was this what it meant to be really rich?

She had just finished unpacking when Jules marched into the bedroom and plonked himself down on the glossy captain's chair.

'Get rid of the suitcases,' he said, without looking up from his BlackBerry. 'Then leave me in peace. I've got to style Nancy for tonight and I need space to get in the vibe.'

It took a few trips to haul all the empty, but surprisingly heavy, Louis Vuitton cases down to a locker on the bottom deck. Then she grabbed her rucksack and hurried back upstairs to look for Marcus.

'Cate – good, there you are.' Marcus was business-like, clutching a notebook and peering into the galley cupboards. 'I want to show you where I buy provisions so that you can shop for me.' He thrust a wicker basket into her hand. 'Cate and I are nipping to the shops,' said Marcus loudly to no one in particular. 'Back later.'

They walked down the gangplank, Marcus loping slowly along, ostentatiously reading from the notebook.

'We need to split up when we get through the arch,' he said urgently, looking ahead as he spoke. 'You head off to the right and walk along by the cafés. Cut back up through the first alleyway and work your way to the top of town. You'll come to the town square eventually and there's a playground. We'll meet there.'

Cate nodded, puzzled, but not inclined to argue.

They passed under the thick city walls and, as they came out into the bright sunshine, Cate immediately struck off to the right, the long, cobbled walkway in front of her edged with cafés and buzzing with the laughter and chat of the lunchtime crowd.

She spotted an alleyway ahead of her. She took a diagonal path, cutting through a café terrace, and headed up into the cool whitewashed alleyway out and away from the noise and bustle of the main street. If Marcus was watching, she had done as he had told her to.

But the quiet stillness of the empty alleyway was making her feel vulnerable and insecure. Why had Marcus sent her this way? She still didn't know if she could trust him. If he had been involved with Andrei's beating, he wouldn't hesitate to get rid of a witness. And she was the only witness there was.

With doubts whizzing through her mind, she turned down into another tiny side street and, at the first doorway she came to, she pushed herself back into the porch so that she could hardly be seen. She waited, her heart beating fast. It seemed almost comical to think that someone would want to follow her, but then the events of the day before hadn't exactly been normal.

The seconds ticked slowly past. Cate was just about to step out of her hiding place when she heard someone coming up the main alleyway. He or she wasn't walking at a normal speed, or even sauntering as a tourist might do. The gait was stealthy, quiet, stop-start. Was it possible that someone really was looking for her?

She waited, her breathing quiet and shallow. Then, nervously, she inched her head forward to look around the door post. Her heart jumped. Just a few metres away from her, a man was walking slowly up and down the alleyway. His face was obscured, but he was tall – over six foot – with large muscular shoulders. Was he looking for her?

Cate drew back into the doorway and held her breath. It looked as if it could be Piot but she daren't stick her head back out again to check. And if it was him, was he friend or foe? She forced herself to stay calm. Either way, she heard his footsteps slowly walk away and, a few minutes later, Cate sidled back down the street and looked carefully around the corner. There was no sign of her blond tracker but she was taking no chances.

Instead of continuing up the alley, she doubled quickly back the way she had come and, knowing that she was safer in a crowd, stayed on the busy high street that led up towards the town square.

The market was finished for the day and the water cannons from the town's cleaning department were hosing away the last of the day's litter. Cate narrowly missed being splashed with dirty water as she walked briskly through. Now the dusty town square was in front of her, the traffic roaring around it at a tremendous rate.

Everyone seemed to be ignoring the pedestrian crossings and Cate felt she had to take her life in her hands just to cross over into the child's playground which dominated the centre of the square.

There was no sign of Marcus. Young children wandered about in the heat, pottering from slide to swing to roundabout, whilst their parents lounged on wooden benches in the shade.

Suddenly Cate thought of Arthur, remembering how cute he was when little and how the two of them had clung together after her mother had suddenly and inexplicably left home.

With a huge effort she brought herself back to the job in hand and, reminded of Arthur and his advice, she sat down on one of the park benches and brought out her phone. She still wasn't sure about these two men and no one knew she was meeting them. She didn't want to overreact but she needed to tell someone where she was going.

She searched around in her rucksack for the tracker device and to her relief found it in a side pocket. She texted Arthur. *Just checking out the tracker. I'll call in one hour.*

Overreacting or not, she felt happier knowing that he was monitoring her. The text sent, she activated the tracker. From now on Arthur would be following her every move – wherever it was she was being led.

Cate stowed the phone back in her rucksack and walked around the edge of the square, skirting the scrubby sand that stood between the playground and the road. She had all but given up looking for Marcus when he appeared through a cluster of trees. He was not alone. By his side was the man who she had just shaken off in the alleyway – it was indeed Piot.

'Well done, Cate,' said Marcus. 'Good work. You completely lost Piot here.'

For a few seconds Cate was speechless. Then she let rip. 'Why was Piot following me?' she demanded. 'You asked me – well, begged me – to help you last night and I told you everything I knew. Now I find that you are playing some stupid game with me. I've had enough, really I have. I'm out of here.'

'Wait, Cate, calm down.' Marcus had her by the arm now. 'Cate, I won't deny we need some help. And we – I – think that you're the ideal person to give us that help. You're clearly brave – you showed that when you saved Andrei's life – and you are great at thinking on your feet.

'Not many sixteen-years-olds are as smart as you. You were right to trust your instincts and confide in me. Shaking off Piot just now – well, that was just a test – and you passed with flying colours.'

Cate's eyes opened wide and she stared from one man to the other. Now she really had no idea what to think. Outrage took over. These men were not being straight with her. Finally she spoke, trying hard to contain her anger. 'Just who the hell are you to be setting me a test?'

Marcus shot Piot a questioning glance. There was a silence and then Piot slowly nodded.

'That, Cate Carlisle,' said Marcus, looking her full in the eye, 'is what you are just about to find out.'

CHAPTER 5

Marcus led Cate back down the hill at a pace so fast she had to jog; her rucksack holding her phone and tracking device bumped comfortably into the small of her back. The trio – Piot behind her – came to a halt outside a fish shop. The fishmonger was still doing a roaring trade.

Today's main catch was sardines, and hundreds of the little fish were piled high in a shimmering pyramid of silvery scales. A middle-aged woman with two tiny children simply held open a large plastic bag by the edge of the counter and one of the fishmongers liberally shovelled in a couple of dozen fish with his bare hands. There was no attempt to weigh the purchase, there was not even a price on the fish, but the shopper seemed to know exactly how much money to hand over and the deal was done without a fuss.

Two large, shiny lobsters, claws still waving, were wrapped up in damp newspaper and shoved into a basket; an old man reached up and helped himself to one of the huge nets of furry mussels which were still dripping pungent sea water. It was a cheerful, colourful spectacle and Cate could have watched it for hours, but Marcus was nudging her shoulder, ushering her down an alleyway by the side of the shop.

A set of rusty iron stairs led steeply up, before turning into a walkway which crossed over the narrow alleyway roughly five metres above them. It was little more than a fire escape, wobbling and clanking slightly as the three of them climbed it in silence. Cate felt calm. She had made her decision to listen to what Marcus was going to say, to trust him and now, she had to admit, she was curious about what she was going to find out.

Ahead, Cate could see a door with dark green, peeling paint marked with a grubby brass plate: *Tomas Bourgoyne. Accountant.*

Piot pushed at the door and it opened into a gloomy corridor, remarkable only for the grubbiest lino Cate had seen in a long time. A door was half open into a tiny office where Cate could just about make out the profile of a dark, curly-headed man focused intently on a computer. He didn't even look up as they passed his door and likewise Marcus and Piot made no sign of recognition. Mr Bourgoyne, Cate presumed. Clearly he was not the person they were coming to see.

As Cate's eyes grew accustomed to the gloom, she spotted the tiny camera lenses positioned at intervals along both sides of the ceiling, whirring through tiny silent arcs following, in perfect synchronicity, the movements of the humans below.

At the far end of the corridor was a door marked *Stocker – Stores*, a door clearly important enough to have been made secure with numerous bolts and locks controlled by a numerical keypad. Cate watched carefully as Marcus, turning half away from her, rapidly punched in a long sequence of numbers.

But Cate was far too quick for him. The keypad was in standard formation, so she could work out from the position of his fingers the keys Marcus had just pressed. Now all she had to do was remember them, and her father had taught Cate and Arthur how to do just that when the three of them were whiling the hours away at yet another airport.

Cate's dad's system went like this. Numbers – make a date and find something that reminds you of it. Marcus had just punched in 1068 – the Battle of Hastings plus two. Switching to the letters on the keys to aid her memory, the next part was CZHH – Christmas in Zambia is Heavy and Hot. Followed by another number sequence: 3110 – Hallowe'en.

The door opened and the three of them walked through to a dark hallway. Opposite them was a lift, the old-fashioned sort with metal folding gates As Cate watched in amazement, Marcus slid aside a filthy panel to reveal a screen no larger than her iPod. He pressed his thumb against it, a green light flickered for a few seconds and then the lift doors slowly opened.

'Welcome aboard,' said Marcus, punching the down button.

The lift juddered and rocked alarmingly before coming to a sudden, almost violent halt. It had covered, Cate reckoned, at least fifty metres, right down into the centre of the massive rock on which Antibes itself stood and certainly deep enough to render Arthur's tracking system useless. She put the thought out of her mind.

There was a protective metal door which had to open before

the trio could leave the lift and, as it began to clank slowly to one side, Cate could see it was a good ten centimetres thick – bulletproof. Wherever she was going, it was somewhere that required full security. Despite her determination to stay cool, her heart was beginning to race. She looked up at Marcus, who seemed like a stranger now, and it took all her will power not to stay in the lift and flee back up and out again to the world of sunshine and blue skies.

He looked back at her and smiled. 'Welcome to the Mediterranean HQ of the International Maritime Intelligence Agency.'

They stepped out into a vast underground space. The air felt thin and sharp, a salty cold hitting at her bare legs and arms and making her shiver.

'What is this place?' she asked in astonishment.

'The caves have been here forever. This part of the world has loads of them,' explained Piot. 'But it took the German High Command to work out that this could be a good place to hide, in the unlikely event that the Allies would invade France from the Mediterranean.

'They put these lifts in and then tunnelled escape routes out through the rocks to the sea at the back of the caves.' His voice took on a sardonic note. 'They happened to have a lot of cheap labour on their hands.'

From one side to another, the area measured at least thirty metres, each high dark wall lit only by the light coming from an almost continuous row of cinema-size screens. In front of many of them stood small groups of men and women either watching the films or bent over computers.

Some screens were blank, emitting a silvery, flickering glow. Others were screening films and, as Cate looked from one to another, she began to recognise what she was seeing.

'Liverpool,' murmered Cate as one film showed running footage of the famous Liver Birds, and the river Mersey.

'Marseilles,' answered Piot for her as she moved her gaze to another screen. 'That's Bremen in Germany; over there is Naples, and look – wonderful Copenhagen. Just like the song. Have you made the link yet?' He grinned at her mischievously. 'Just how good is your geography?'

'All ports,' said Cate slowly. 'But why?'

'A-ha, well done,' said Piot cheerfully. 'International crime usually involves things like drugs and people and goods, and all these need to be moved around. Planes, even the small ones, have to file a flight plan and the large ones, well, let's just say they have caught more drug dealers since the security operations were brought in after 9/11 than in the whole of the twentieth century. Cars and lorries, forget it. A random road check or a sniffer dog at a border crossing can destroy the best laid plans. No, even in this day and age you can't beat a nice fast boat when it comes to shifting illegal items efficiently. And all boats have to come into port at one time or another.'

'Which is where the IMIA comes in,' Marcus joined in. 'This section keeps an eye on every major port from the Atlantic Ocean to the Black Sea. No one knows us, but we're there. We watch and track and chase and finally we step in and sabotage anything nasty, before it happens.

'In short, we do the dirty work that the local police can't, or don't even know about, and that the military haven't got the expertise for. We go undercover, sometimes for months at a time. We break rules, use guns and surveillance and now . . .' He grinned at Cate. '. . . even teenagers.'

'You won't have heard of us, of course. Nor will any politicians – or they won't admit to it, which comes to the same thing. We're on our own, really, and that's the way we like it.'

As Marcus finished talking, Cate suddenly realised that they had been joined by a fourth person. He was not much taller than Cate, his dark hair receding, but he nevertheless carried with him an unmistakable aura of authority and power.

Not be messed with, thought Cate as the two of them sized each other up in silence.

Marcus broke the impasse. 'Cate, this is Henri Sorenzki, ex-SAS, seconded to the American CIA, had a jaunt with Mossad, back as number two at Interpol, and now Head of the Southern Central Sector of the IMIA. Got all that?' He grinned as Cate gaped in amazement.

'And Henri,' continued Marcus, 'meet your latest recruit. Fluent in several languages, can get by in a few more. Trained in martial arts, has natural survival skills and is one of the bravest teenagers I have ever met. She may be young but she already thinks and acts like an agent. She's a natural.'

There was silence. Then Henri spoke. 'Prove it,' he said, his black eyes staring into Cate's face. To her surprise, his accent was cut-glass British public school.

Cate felt a flicker of self-doubt before her competitive streak kicked in. 'Well,' she said in Russian, 'if I wanted to get back in here I know that the code is 106829443110.'

Marcus looked rueful. 'I did it very quickly,' he said to no one in particular.

'And?' said Henri.

Cate looked at her watch. This time she spoke in Italian. 'If I don't make a phonecall within the next hour, then you are going to have the local *gendarmes* racing to break down the door of the poor accountant upstairs – which is probably where the last reading was given off by my tracking device. They might not find me but they'll make life difficult for you.'

A look of annoyance flitted across Henri's face. 'Marcus, this is a security breach.'

'Sorry, Henri,' said Marcus, sounding not very sorry at all. 'I told you she was good.'

Henri sighed. 'OK, Marcus, I believe you. But she's just a kid, no matter how bright or tough she is. What happens if she gets hurt or, worse still, jeopardises our work?'

'We don't have a choice,' said Marcus, no longer smiling. 'We're going nowhere fast on this case using orthodox methods and we have already lost one good man and Andrei is fighting for his life in hospital. Thanks to Cate, we found him just in time, but he's in a coma and hasn't spoken since.'

Cate looked up at the mention of Andrei but Marcus was in full flow.

'Now our intelligence shows that the latest shipment has arrived and we probably have less than a week before it disappears out again. If that happens, who knows when we'll get a good chance to crack the case again?

'Cate is in the right place, at the right time, to help us and no one will ever suspect a kid like her of being an agent. She is our best hope of working out what the hell is going on here.'

There was a silence. Three pairs of eyes turned to Henri, but still he hesitated. Then Marcus played his trump card.

'I heard the American President has taken a special interest in the case,' he said slyly. 'Apparently he's very keen on preserving endangered animals. He is talking about bringing in the CIA.'

Henri went visibly pale under his dark skin. 'OK, Marcus, you win. But just for this case, you understand? After that we debrief her and she goes back to her old life, gossiping about boys on Facebook or whatever it is girls do nowadays. And keep this quiet, on a need- to-know only. Even within our own department. You understand? I don't want anyone else to know that we're working with kids. We'll be a bloody laughing stock.'

He shook his head, as if in disbelief at his rashness, but still held out his hand to Cate. 'Welcome aboard, Cate Carlisle. And good luck.'

'Just hang on a minute,' said Cate, ignoring the outstretched hand and glaring first at Marcus and then at Henri. 'Is anyone going to actually ask my opinion about this? More to the point, could one of you please tell me exactly what is going on?'

She spoke with such vehemence that two men at a desk ten metres or so away looked up in amazement before turning back to a map on their computer.

'You bring me here, put me on some sort of trial, discuss just how good I am, right under my nose, and not one of you has the decency to even ask me what I want to do. You're acting worse than parents!

'Why would I agree to just jump in with you without

knowing what for? I'd be mad to do that – and come to that, you'd be mad to let me.'

There was a sharp intake of breath from Marcus and Piot. Henri glowered at Cate, who glowered back.

'Tell her,' said Henri abruptly. 'Then get her to work.'

Silently, Marcus and Piot walked towards a desk which was standing underneath a screen showing footage of what looked like little more than a shanty town. Children were standing knee-deep in rubbish and mean-looking young men were hanging out at street corners. Most of the buildings were little more than shacks, some with tin roofs, a few like concrete bunkers. A couple of chickens wandered down what passed for a street and some mangy dogs were scavenging through the rubbish.

'Right, Cate, we don't have much time,' Marcus said abruptly. 'Concentrate while I talk you through the case. You can give us your answer afterwards.

'This is Tendo, which believe it or not is the capital of the West African state of Ramibia. Heard of it?'

Cate shook her head. 'Never,' she said.

'No real reason why you should have. Ramibia is an ex-French colony spread across a few thousand kilometres of sand which runs along the West Coast of Africa. One of the poorest countries in the world, most kids your age there will have kids of their own and will be dead by the time they are forty-five.

'The worst place to live in Ramibia is Tendo. It's a port, but not in any sense that you would recognise. Fifty years ago, Tendo was a vital part of the major trade routes in and out of West Africa, a huge well-oiled cog in a very busy wheel.

'Today it's a hell-hole, rife with pirates and thugs of every nationality and description,' Marcus said grimly. 'There are mercenaries from Angola, terrorist groups from Pakistan, money men from Uzbekistan and the place is run like a private fiefdom.

'The harbour master has his own helicopter and bodyguards and the mayor controls a small army, complete with, rumour has it, a couple of tanks, just in case anyone is brave enough to try and come and arrest him.

'You can imagine what goes through the port today. Illegal drugs, trafficked people, fake pharmaceuticals, missile parts, stolen credit cards – even parts of nuclear bombs have been known to turn up. It's like the Wild West, only with Sat-nav and missile launchers. Even the CIA pulled out last year. But we've still got some men in there, brave sods that they are. And one of them sent us footage of something that was pretty awful. Which is where we – and you – come in.'

Marcus picked up a pair of headsets, nodded for Cate to do the same, then pressed a button on the remote and the screen went blank. A split second later, it lit up again and the shanty town had gone. This time the camera was in a dark, confined space, moving shakily and hesitantly from side to side. There was no sound except a few small, sharp intakes of breath from the person holding the camera. A sound, Cate thought, of fear.

The camera focused on a tiny cage, which at first appeared to be empty. But then, as the camera zoomed in, Cate spotted a creature lying at the back of the cage. Startled by the camera, it turned its head and Cate saw, with horror, that it was a baby orang-utan. She had never seen such a pitiful creature. Vomit streaked the front of its chest, most of its fur was matted or missing and its eyes were inflamed and full of pus. A large gash could clearly be seen along its back and its limbs were trembling either through pain, fear, or both.

As it saw the cameraman, the wretched creature pushed itself further back into its cell, scrabbling crablike in a desperate circle, before giving up and crouching back down in silent misery.

The camera left the cage and moved on to the next one. Another distressed animal, this time an infant snow leopard, lay in the stifling darkness, without bedding or, as far as Cate could see, water or food. Next to it, panting and wheezing, was a Siberian tiger cub, its distinctive stripes almost unrecognisable under a layer of what looked like excrement. Cate felt sick. She wanted to look away but she couldn't.

Cate had always loved animals, even though her nomadic lifestyle had meant she was never able to have a pet of her own, and it was clear that these poor creatures were going through a trauma too awful to contemplate.

Despite herself, Cate felt tears stinging behind her eyes. 'Get a grip,' she told herself crossly.

'Do you want to see any more?' Marcus asked her quietly.

Cate turned to him. 'No, I get the gist,' she said roughly, trying to hide her emotions. 'What's going on? Why are these animals being kept like this? What are they doing in Tendo?'

'We don't really have the answer to those questions,' said Marcus. 'Animal poaching has always been a problem, you probably know that. Over the twentieth century we lost hundreds of thousands of elephants, gorillas, tigers, and that is still going on. But now the really rare species – the Siberian tiger and the orang-utan, the ones on the verge of extinction – well, they are much more protected.

'Most of them live in reserves which are guarded and protected 24/7 with CCTV and often watchtowers. They are looked after by teams of conservationists, people who are very dedicated and very, very protective. At any one time they more or less know the whereabouts of every single one of their charges, and big money is spent making sure they don't lose them to the bad guys. It's worked well. The populations of these species are slowly but surely increasing, although we all know it's going to take a long time.'

'But now?' asked Cate.

'Exactly,' said Marcus. 'But now, these animals, the ones that you saw and dozens of others, are being taken from right under the noses of their protectors and disappearing. They're young, as you saw, all tagged and microchipped. We're losing a dozen or so a month from across Asia, Africa, even the Chinese are reporting that their giant pandas have been stolen. That's no mean feat. The Chinese government would cheerfully execute anyone who harmed a hair of their precious pandas' heads.

'Whoever is doing this is playing a very high risk game in some of the most dangerous countries in the world. We can pretty much guess that the smuggling is being carried out for financial gain – it always is. But is someone out there trying to build up a private zoo, or using them for some nonsensical medicinal purpose that we haven't yet come across? We just don't know who is behind it or why.

'But we do know that whoever it is, they are clearly

extremely well organised, well funded and know exactly what they want.'

Cate was puzzled. 'You said the animals are disappearing, but you know where the film was taken. And that it's somewhere in Tendo, which is why you're monitoring it so closely.' She pointed at the screen. 'So, why can't you just charge in and rescue them?'

'If only it were that simple.' Marcus sounded frustrated and weary. 'For months we knew that they were going missing but had no idea where they had gone. There was no chatter on the internet, they didn't turn up in any of the usual dodgy dealers' hotspots, or on websites that trade in these things. They just vanished into thin air.

'That was until last month, when we received this film from one of our undercover guys. He'd discovered these animals waiting in Tendo to go on a ship bound for – yes, Cate – Antibes.'

'Why didn't he call the police and get them to raid the place?' Cate was bewildered.

Marcus sighed. 'Because he knew just how corrupt the local cops are. But he was rumbled anyhow and he hasn't been seen since. This is Tendo, remember. The poor sod is probably lying at the bottom of Tendo harbour, hugging a concrete block. That is, if he's lucky.'

Suddenly the room, and the world, seemed to be a colder, scarier place. Cate shuddered.

'Somehow, he managed to get a message to his IMIA handler and tell him where he had hidden the data card that held the film file,' continued Piot.

'Who was his handler?' asked Cate, although she already had a pretty good idea.

'Yes, it was Andrei,' said Piot soberly. 'He was trailed back to Antibes where he was attacked and, if it wasn't for you, would probably be dead.'

'Clearly whoever is running this operation knows someone is on to them,' broke in Marcus.

'We have to stop these thefts. Not only are we losing too many precious creatures but we have no idea what is being done to them. At this rate, some of these species could be facing extinction. Gone, forever.'

There was silence. Then Cate took a deep breath. 'OK, I understand all that,' she said quietly. 'It's terrible, it's . . . disgusting, it's revolting.' She struggled to find the words. 'But where do I come in? If they are in Antibes, those animals could be anywhere.'

Marcus and Piot exchanged glances.

'We don't have much to go on but we do have one lead,' said Piot. 'Animals often disappear when Nancy Kyle comes visiting. It happened in China, Thailand, in Nepal, in South Africa, Rwanda and Kenya. She turns up, big fanfare, talk on animal rights, donates money for conservation, an orphanage whatever, sometimes adopts a small child for the heck of it and then, nine times out of ten, an animal goes missing. And now that the trail is leading to Antibes, she turns up right here, out of the blue, when she was actually scheduled to be in London for the entire Wimbledon fortnight.'

'But this is Nancy Kyle we're talking about,' said Cate, horrified. 'She loves animals, campaigns for them, raises money for them. God, she has saved thousands of them. Why on earth would she be involved in something as awful as this?'

'It doesn't make sense, I agree,' said Marcus calmly. 'But either it's one huge coincidence – and personally I don't much believe in coincidences – or Nancy Kyle is involved in the sort of devious double bluff not seen since the end of the Cold War.'

'Those were the days,' said Piot dreamily.

Marcus glared at him. He turned back to Cate and looked at her, almost pleadingly. 'Cate, you're right at the epicentre of this whole thing. And the beauty is, no one will ever suspect you of being anything other than, well, a kid. You can find out so much more than we ever could. Just hang out near Nancy, find out things about her, snoop around, keep close to her. She could be completely innocent, but I'm sure she's the key to cracking this case. And you're the best person to help us do that.'

And if I decide that this is all too big for me, too scary, then what? thought Cate, staring at Marcus's intense expression.

The agent seemed to read her mind and shrugged. 'Cate, if you don't want to do this, just tell us. We're not monsters or modern day Fagins, forcing you to do something against your will. Say the word and we'll get you away from here and we'll never mention it again.' His voice took on a wheedling tone. 'Why don't you look on it as a charitable endeavour, or a sort of really unusual work experience? Help us out if you can and, at the end of it, you just walk away. Well, Cate, what will it be?'

CHAPTER 6

Cate stumbled back out of the alleyway into the bright, late afternoon sunshine and stood for a few minutes, gulping in the fresh air, frantically trying to reset her brain and make sense of what she had just agreed to do.

Gradually, the heat warmed her cold limbs, the fresh, salty sea breeze blowing away the cloying dampness of the caves from her nostrils, and she began to feel part of the human race again.

She looked down at the bulging straw shopping baskets she was clutching in either hand. Marcus had shoved them at her just before he sent her back to rejoin the outside world. 'Your cover,' he had said. 'Take them back to the boat and carry on as normal.'

But nestled in her pocket was another far more interesting gift from her new colleague.

'Gadgets, devices, tricks of the trade,' Marcus had told her with a big grin as he handed her the innocuous-looking square tin. 'Every good spy should have them. There's another gadget in the bottom of one the baskets too. I'll run through all of them with you later.'

Then he was gone, back into the murky depths of the cave. As the lift screeched and juddered its way upwards, Cate wondered how someone who did a job like Marcus's could manage to behave in an even remotely normal way, let alone be that laid-back on the boat. She knew it must be tough to compartmentalise like this.

'Think like an agent, act like an agent,' she told herself as she sent Arthur a text to tell him she was safe and well, and deactivated the tracker. That done, she began to walk back down the cobbled street towards the marina.

Back on the boat, no one seemed to have noticed that Cate had even been away. Wendy was on the middle deck, quietly chatting to Lulu who was sprawled out full length on one of the large sofas. Both women gave Cate a cursory glance and a wave, noting, Cate hoped, her shopping baskets.

She unpacked the baskets in the galley, marvelling as she saw delicacies such as Beluga Caviar, dressed crab and fresh lobster. Right at the bottom was a small package with her name on it. She took it, and headed down to her cabin and shut the door on the world with relief.

She lay on the bed and forced herself to think hard. Were these people for real? Or were they the type of grown men who play-acted at being soldiers on paintballing weekends or wore khaki to the pub and claimed to have been in the SAS? If so, it was a pretty elaborate scam, especially considering the vast underground operation that she had just witnessed.

But Marcus and Henri didn't seem that type. Then there was the small matter of Andrei and his beating. She had certainly witnessed real thuggery, real criminals at work.

She needed to find out more and there was just one person she could really trust to help her. She pulled out her laptop and, remembering Marcus's advice to cover her tracks at all time, input the code Arthur had given her to activate the signal scrambler he'd set up. From now on, anyone trying to track her down using her internet access would be unable to pinpoint just where she was. She was, in cyber sense, invisible.

She waited as the computer connected to the web, then angled the camera towards her face. She found herself praying that Arthur would be sitting in his bedroom, close enough to hear the computer alert calling him. She suddenly craved the sound of his voice, the sound of home and normality, and for the second time that day felt tears pricking at the back of her eyes.

To her utter relief her prayers were answered. Within seconds, Arthur's face was on her screen, a big smile pasted across his face.

'Hi, sis.' His voice sounded clear on the screen. 'What's happening?'

'God, Arthur, where do I start?' Cate swallowed hard. 'I miss you so much.' She fell silent.

The smile on Arthur's face disappeared. 'Sis, what's wrong? Are you OK?'

For a few awful seconds Cate thought she really was going to break down. She took a deep breath. 'Arthur,' she began, 'can you record this for me, put it on a memory stick and keep it somewhere safe?'

He nodded, not quite understanding why, but obediently he tapped a few buttons on his keyboard and then signalled for her to go ahead.

'I'm in the middle of something,' she said quietly. 'A mystery, a crime, an investigation. I don't quite know how it happened, and part of me doesn't believe it is for real, but somehow, well, it is.'

As she began to recount the events of the last two days, Cate was well aware how fantastic they must have sounded. She could see Arthur's green eyes growing wider and the colour draining from his cheeks.

He let her talk, listening carefully without interruption. When she had finished he took a deep breath. 'Sis, are you safe?'

'I am for now.' She found herself smiling. 'Although I'm starting to doubt everything. I thought this boat was safe, home even, but now I'm beginning to wonder.'

'Look, Cate,' said Arthur, 'what's happened to you sounds like something out of a Jason Bourne film. Like you've landed in the middle of some great fantastic adventure. But it won't be so great if you get hurt. And these guys that you're dealing with, well, both sides sound pretty hardcore to me.'

'I'll have a look at Ramibia, especially that port – what was it called? Tendo?' Arthur was immediately distracted from his concern for Cate by the thought of some juicy cyber-detecting. 'Tendo's mayor and the harbour master – they're the two people we want to know about,' continued Arthur, almost to himself. 'They must have internet access and email maybe, even if they are hidden away somewhere in the deepest, darkest ends of the web. I can try and get into their systems and see what I can find out.'

Now Cate was worried. 'Arthur, be careful. These are really heavy people. If they suspect you are spying on them, well, they could get pretty angry. You don't want them tracking you down.'

Arthur smiled confidently. 'Cate, the day someone can track me down over the internet is the day I hang up my mouse and look forward to working at McDonalds. This is *me* you're talking to. Don't you remember that time I got into the payroll system and doubled Dad's salary? They never did find out how that happened. Or when I got the final chapters of *The Deathly Hallows* way before anyone else. Now that was a mean piece of work.'

'OK, OK, Arthur, you're the best.' Cate was laughing now. 'But if you think for one second that someone is on to you, then promise me, swear to me on Dad's life, that you will get out of there and cover your tracks as you go. It's vital that they don't trace you.'

'I promise, sis, but I want you to promise me something in return.' His face was completely serious now. 'Text or mail me the code I'm sending you now every morning at ten a.m. and evening at ten p.m. I will give you an hour's leeway. After that, if I don't hear from you, I'll hand over this memory stick to Dad or Monique and let them come after you. Is that fair?'

'Not only is it fair, Arthur, it's genius. As Dad always says, a back-up plan is a good plan.'

Brother and sister grinned at each other through

cyberspace. Cate's phone pinged. She had Arthur's code.

'And look into those wildlife reserves that guard the really precious animals. Somehow security has been breached in every one of them and I just don't know how that can happen.'

'Everyone has their price,' said Arthur solemnly.

'Arthur!' said Cate half shocked, half laughing. 'When did you get so cynical?'

He grinned back. 'I've been watching too much *EastEnders* again.'

'Just tune into me every night,' said Cate happily. Arthur always managed to cheer her up. 'It's like a soap opera here, I can tell you. There's Nancy Kyle looking like a goddess, phone calls from pop stars, a weirdo stylist who also does her horoscope and a really scary woman who, as far as I can tell, just hangs around answering her BlackBerry.'

'Sounds great,' said Arthur enthusiastically. 'I'm going to talk Dad into bringing me down to see you once school ends. In the meantime, have you actually gone to sea yet?'

'Er, no.' Cate laughed. 'I'm beginning to realise that owning a yacht doesn't actually have much to do with sailing. In fact, I wouldn't be surprised if Nancy Kyle suffered from seasickness!'

As both of them howled with laughter there was a knocking at Cate's cabin door.

'Cate?' It was Wendy. 'I need a hand. Tass Taplinski has rocked into town and Nancy wants to make sure he has an evening to remember.'

Cate motioned to Arthur to be quiet.

'Cate,' said Wendy again, this time more impatiently. 'Are you in there? Can you hear me?'

'Yup, yes,' said Cate, trying her best to sound as if she had just woken up. 'Just having a little nap. I'll be up in ten minutes.'

'Make it five,' said Wendy shortly. 'We've got a whole heap of things to do.'

Cate waited a few seconds before resuming her conversation with Arthur, but this time in a whisper.

'Phew,' said her brother. 'She sounds fierce.'

'She's all right really,' Cate told him. 'She just has a lot to do. Anyway, see what I mean about a soap opera? Now, to top it all, the gorgeous Tass Taplinski, darling of the celebrity magazines, the man who has dated just about every desirable woman from Madonna to Princess Mary of Lithuania, is about to come into my life.'

Arthur giggled. 'Tass Taplinski, eh? It says here he won Top Pecs of the Year in *Cosmo* magazine three years running,' he said, reading from the web as he talked. 'Plus his dad is the fourth richest man in Russia.'

'He's more than just a pretty face,' said Cate defensively. 'He played pro tennis.'

'Reached the dizzy heights of number 247 in the world rankings,' said Arthur gleefully.

'He produced that film, what was it called? *Bloodlines of the Father.*'

'Which received a Raspberry Award for being so rubbish,' said Arthur still reading. 'And he has been arrested for drink-driving in LA, been investigated for tax fraud in Germany. Uh-oh, and it says here Daddy had to bail him out of a bankruptcy suit in Florida when his property company hit the skids.'

'Arthur, stop it,' laughed Cate. 'He's a pretty hot loser, anyway. A loser with his own yacht, a plane, a Mayfair apartment in London and a house in LA. I just want to get close enough to smell his aftershave and get our pic taken together so I can show my mates. Listen, I've got to go. Love you lots.'

'You too, sis. And don't worry. I'll get to work for you straightaway. By this time tomorrow I'll know everything there is to know about the IMIA, Ramibia and Nancy Kyle. Leave it to your clever little bro.'

Cate hurried off to Wendy. She found her talking to Bill on the outside deck.

Wendy thrust a tray holding drinks into Cate's hands. 'Would you ask Nancy what she wants for dinner and when.'

Carrying the heavy tray, Cate went back inside the boat, and padded quietly through the salon towards the master suite. As she got nearer to Nancy's cabin, she heard music playing and the sound of raucous laughter.

Cate tapped quietly at the door and waited for half a minute or so before rapping again, this time slightly louder. Still the music continued and Cate gingerly opened the door with her left hand while trying to keep the tray level with her right.

The room was almost unrecognisable from the immaculate space where, just a few hours earlier, Cate had carefully unpacked the cases. Now most of those clothes were strewn over the bed, some of them trampled on the floor. A plate of cold chips was balanced precariously on the vanity sink.

Piled on the pillows were a host of giant cuddly toys – a panda, a tiger, a lion and a gorilla. There was even a white cheetah with a grotesque giant pink heart strung around its neck bearing the words *exotic and rare. Significant?* wondered Cate. *Or normal for someone who's still not yet quite grown up? Is that true of Nancy?*

She took a deep breath, unsure as to whether she would be bawled out or made welcome.

'Hi,' she said, looking around the room for Nancy. She raised her voice nervously 'I've brought your drinks. Shall I pour you them?'

As she spoke, the supermodel came wandering out of the bathroom, wearing a very short, lemon silk dressing gown and an enormous pair of diamond stud earrings. Even with her red hair wet and tousled and without any make-up, she looked sensational, her green eyes wide and bright and her skin palely luminous.

She was clutching her mobile phone to her left ear as she walked and her foghorn laugh filled the room. 'Darling . . .' She sounded excited. 'You know I love you, but Tass has just arrived in town and he has to come first. I'll try to get him along but he does get sooo jealous when he has to share little old me. Remember what happened in New York? And me such a good girl and all.'

Her caller obviously made the right reply because there was that laugh again. Cate tried hard not to wince. She would need earplugs if she was going to stay around Nancy for much longer.

'Good job Tass didn't hear that or he'd set one of his bodyguards on you,' cackled Nancy. 'Anyway, babe, have to go and make myself look beautiful for my billionaire. I'll party another time with my lovely Oirish boys, so I will. Promise. Love you loads. *Ciao, ciao.*'

She put her phone down.

'Put it there.' She gestured to the dressing table without even looking at Cate. 'There, babe, there,' she said more impatiently as Cate hesitated.

Remembering what Marcus had said, Cate thought desperately of a conversation opener. 'What are you wearing tonight?' she asked timidly.

'Dunno, babe.' Nancy, who was sitting on the bed checking the glossy black varnish on her toenails, sounded vaguely shocked at Cate's initiative.

Cate ploughed bravely on. 'I unpacked all your stuff today. It was – amazing.'

This time Nancy looked up. 'Oh yeah, right, er, thanks.' She looked at Cate properly for the first time. 'Tell you what, babe. You probably know what clothes I've brought better than I do, and I'm not sure about what Jules has chosen for tonight. So you tell me what to wear for my gorgeous fella. Something sexy but not too slinky. Definitely not tarty, blingy sexy. He can get that anytime from a Russian girl if he wants it. No, I have to look classy.'

'You couldn't look anything else,' said Cate and this time she meant the compliment. 'But I do think you look fab in midnight blue. It sort of sets your hair off and makes your skin glow.'

For a minute Cate thought she might have overdone the compliments. But Nancy was delighted.

'Clever,' said the supermodel approvingly. 'I can see we're gonna be great mates.' She leant into the pile of clothes on the bed and pulled out a dark blue sleeveless shift and held it against her slender frame. The neckline was high and demure but to make up for that, the floaty hem wafted somewhere only just below her knicker line.

With a deft movement she slithered out one foot and then another and suddenly she was standing in the smallest sliver of silver wedged sandals which added another four inches to her already giraffe-like legginess.

'It's gorgeous,' said Cate, gaping. 'It's perfect. Then just a silver bracelet and some really long earrings and you're pretty much done.'

'Blimey, babe,' Nancy sat back down on the bed. 'Well, that's another favour you've done me today. Me and Jules usually spend hours working out what to wear. What am I going to do with myself? Read a book?'

She laughed, her wide generous mouth curving open as she threw back her head in real enjoyment and suddenly she was transformed from a sulky sophisticate to something approaching a normal young woman.

There was a sharp tap at the door and Nancy's smile faded. Without a word, Lulu bustled into the cabin, her quick efficient gaze taking in the shambolic mess and, Cate was sure, the friendly vibe between herself and Nancy.

'Oh my God, Nancy, you're not thinking of wearing *that,* are you?' Lulu said sharply, her accent sounding stronger than ever in the small space. 'You wore that dress two weeks ago in New York at the Museum of Fashion event. Your picture was everywhere, simply everywhere. Do you want Tass to laugh at you, to think you are a cheap woman who wears the same things again and again? This is how you compete with the daughters of billionaires? Put it down, put it down now.'

Cate was cringing with embarrassment. She waited with baited breath for Nancy to lay into Lulu. But instead the supermodel looked tired and deflated. 'Sorry,' she mumbled. 'I forgot. Thanks, Lulu.'

Lulu was now stalking triumphantly around the cabin, picking up clothes and shoes and taking them through to the walk-in wardrobe. As she did so, Cate spotted something very odd. There were many pictures of children – Nancy's brood Cate presumed – adorning the walls. But, on the bedside table stood a cluster of silver framed photographs featuring Nancy with various animals – rare animals: a Siberian tiger, a giant turtle, a silver-back gorilla, taken at locations ranging from what looked like a rainforest, to a mountainside, to the bluest of oceans. Cate tried to move closer to the pictures to get a better look, but as she did so Lulu came back into the cabin and let rip at her.

'What are you still doing here?' she barked. 'You're in the way. Go.'

Cate shot a glance at Nancy, but she had her back turned and was looking around the wardrobe. Cate realised that Nancy had forgotten all about her. As she left the room she made a mental note to find a way back in there for a thorough search as soon as possible.

As she passed the kitchen, she saw that Marcus had finally returned. He had his back to the door and was hard at work flambéing a hunk of meat over a very lively flame. She paused, uncertain as to whether she should talk to him or ignore him. She decided that the first course of action would be the most natural. 'Hey, Marcus,' she called out. 'How're you doing?'

Marcus turned and grinned at her. The transformation was extraordinary. Gone was the taut-faced Marcus of just a few hours earlier and in his place was the laid-back chef. 'Thanks for bringing the shopping back,' said Marcus. 'Any orders for tonight from the boss?'

'Don't think so,' said Cate. 'But I really didn't get a chance to ask her. I think she just wants something romantic for her and Tass.'

'Leave it to Marcus,' he said, winking at her. 'Food and romance, they're my two favourite words in the whole of the world.'

Cate, still stunned at his ability to switch personalities so easily and convincingly, made her escape and went to look for Wendy.

'What can I do to help, Wendy?' she asked, when she found the steward up on the top deck by the pool. The afternoon sun was finally losing its burn and the heat was pleasant and soothing. Smells of garlic and frying steaks were beginning to drift out from the other boats in the marina.

'Mmmm. Well, Tass is due in about half an hour,' said Wendy, folding the thick towels with origami-like precision and placing them on the ends of the sun loungers. 'He'll bring bodyguards with him – his dad insists on it – and they'll need feeding. I guess I'll do the main waiting up here and you bring the drinks then go down and look after the bodyguards. You'll be on call until Tass and Nancy go out and party or turn in for the night. Either way, I'll do the late shift this time in case they want anything in the night. Your turn next time.'

'Fair enough,' said Cate. A thought struck her. 'Shall I tidy

Nancy's room while she's out on deck?' she said carefully. 'It was a bit of a shambles earlier.'

'Thanks, Cate, if you're not too tired that'd be great.' Wendy sounded pleased and slightly touched, and for a few seconds Cate felt a pang of guilt that she was not exactly offering because she was feeling helpful. 'But if she wants to go back into the room for any reason you have to leave it immediately. Be careful.'

Don't worry, thought Cate, her heart racing at the thought of her first ever spying assignment. *You have no idea how careful I'll be.*

There was a clatter of footsteps on the pontoon below and the two of them rushed to peer over the polished timber handrails. Beneath them on the pontoon stood three men. Two were tall, easily topping six foot four and dwarfing the smaller man who stood between them.

'They're early,' said Wendy through a gritted smile as she waved to them.

One of the bodyguards was very broad, his shoulders straining out from an oversized beige jacket and his thick neck almost as wide as his closely shaven blond head. As Cate looked him up and down she spotted a bulge around the left waist of his dark blue chinos, scarcely concealed by the jacket he was wearing.

Armed, thought Cate. The other man was as dark as his companion was blond. Dark skinned, dark hair cut in a similar but slightly less severe manner than his colleague. He was dressed all in black: black T-shirt, jeans and leather ankle boots. The entire effect was one, Cate thought, of a pantomime villain. But any urge to snigger at his appearance quickly faded when Cate spotted that he too was armed and this time there was no attempt to cover up what looked like a pistol equipped with a silencer. *An assassin's weapon*, Cate thought with a shiver, and shot a sideways glance at Wendy to see if she had noticed. But her boss seemed oblivious.

'Good evening, Tass,' she called down to the smallest of the three men below. 'Great to see you. Welcome aboard.'

Without waiting to witness his raised hand of acknowledgment, she moved quickly towards the spiral staircase and disappeared down them at double-quick pace with Cate following at a distance.

As they reached the boarding deck, they saw that the two bodyguards had already put on deck shoes and were striding purposefully up the gangplank. Cate took a deep breath as they came towards her.

'Welcome aboard,' she said with her best smile. 'I'm Cate and I will be happy to help you.'

Both men inclined their heads politely as they walked past her. 'I'm Mikey,' said the tall blond-haired man with a distinctly Cockney accent. His pale blue eyes were expressionless and he had the sort of bland face that was hard to remember, a face that would blend easily into a crowd and be hard to describe after he had gone. 'And my mate 'ere is Ahmed. He don't speak much English but he's good wiv a gun.'

Ahmed turned a pair of very pale green eyes on Cate and then passed over her dismissively.

'Nice to meet you, Cate, and fanks for the welcome,' continued Mikey. 'But don't worry, luv, we've been 'ere before.

We know where everyfing is and we'll make ourselves comfortable. Now if you don't mind, we'll just check out the boat for anything untoward. In our own time.'

Cate looked uncertainly towards Wendy who was at the bottom of the gangplank exchanging kisses with Tass then nodded at her. 'Whatever, Cate,' she said. 'Just let them get on with it. They've got a job to do protecting their boss.'

Suddenly Cate felt a lurch of panic. The gun was still tucked carefully under her bed, a place that no doubt the men would look first. She had a sickening feeling that she had been terribly, stupidly, careless not to have dealt with this problem before.

Cate turned to the men and in desperation she watched them as they set off to the top deck.

Cate had to get to her cabin now, but as she tried to make her escape she heard Wendy calling her back.

'Cate. Cate, this is Tass Taplinski.'

Reluctantly, Cate turned back and then had to stop her jaw from dropping. She had seen pictures of Tass over the years, coming out of nightclubs with a gorgeous woman on his arm, at Ascot, Wimbledon and the Stowe Ball, and of course the latest shots of him at various social events with Nancy Kyle. But, Cate realised, those pictures which had shown him to be a good-looking guy had hardly done him justice. Standing in front of her, gazing into her face with his extraordinary almond-shaped blue-black eyes was one of the most handsome men she had ever seen in her life.

Strong wavy hair curled over olive-tinted skin and, despite the fact that he had not played on the tennis circuit for almost five years, he still had the physical tautness and toned hardness of a professional athlete. He was around five foot ten, Cate guessed, but his broad shoulders and narrow hips made him look much taller.

There was, thought Cate, something almost fake in his perfection, as if he had been airbrushed into looking that good. He belonged on the pages of magazines and in the movies – not here standing in front of her. She sighed inwardly.

To her annoyance, Cate felt almost breathless as she shook his hand and she guessed he knew the effect he was having on her.

'Well hello, Cate,' he drawled in an accent that was an attractive mix between his native Russian and North American. 'It's very good to meet you. It's always great to have new people around and if Wendy recommends you – well, any friend of hers is a friend of mine!'

He turned to Wendy and anyone could see the effect his words were having on her – she smiled adoringly at him. That made Cate want to giggle.

Get a grip girl, she thought. *He's a smug poser who loves himself far too much.*

'I know where to come if I need anything,' said Tass, turning back to Cate. 'And now, if you two ladies will excuse me, I must go to see the gorgeous Nancy. *Ciao, ciao* for now.'

He headed through the glass doors and towards the master suite. But before he could take more than a few steps, there was a huge scream as a whirl of energy flung herself into his arms.

'Darling, Tass!' It was Nancy, immaculately dishevelled and

smelling of Chanel No 5. 'What kept you so long, you naughty boy?'

Taking his hand she led him back into the salon of the boat. Wendy heaved an audible sigh and Cate shot her a sympathetic glance.

But she had more pressing concerns on her mind. The gun had to be hidden and hidden quickly.

'Wendy,' she said. 'Now everyone's on board do you mind if I have a quick break to freshen up and have something to eat before we start serving dinner. Is that OK?'

Wendy, still in a dreamlike state, waved her hand vaguely and Cate shot off down below decks. To her relief, the bodyguards had not yet made their way to the crew quarters. She thought fast. It was way too late to hand the gun into the police and she didn't want to just pitch it overboard in case it somehow got washed ashore.

She had to be honest with herself. The events of the last two days meant that she actually liked the thought of having a gun around. It was her protection if the worst came to the worst. She shook her head, amazed at how much her world – and her attitudes – had changed in just a few days.

Cate suddenly had a brainwave. She headed to the mess room and opened the small chest freezer in the kitchenette. A few seconds of rummaging around and she had what she was looking for – a packet of frozen vegetables. Her heart racing, she double checked that the corridor was still empty and nipped back into her room, fished the gun from under the bed and slipped it inside her T-shirt.

No one ever eats brussels sprouts, she thought to herself as she slid the pistol inside the packet of stubby vegetables. She pushed it right down to the bottom of the freezer. 'And no one ever looks more than three quarters of the way down a freezer.'

She was just re-arranging the chips and frozen burgers over the gun when she heard a noise in the corridor. The bodyguards were on their way. For an instant she panicked, but then, as the steps drew nearer, she reached for a frozen dish marked *Chicken curry*. A few seconds later, as the bodyguards walked stealthily into the room, she was sitting at the bench gazing at the whirring microwave.

'Starving,' she said brightly. Her heart was racing, petrified by just how close she had come to disaster.

The two men nodded in return and got to work carrying out a thorough search of the mess room, checking the TV cables and behind the pictures on the walls.

To Cate's horror, Ahmed lifted up the lid of the freezer and had a quick look inside, moving a few bits of food around. But the gun stayed hidden.

'Fanks,' said Mikey over his shoulder as he left the room, the only word either of the men had spoken since they came in. Friendliness was clearly not their priority.

The microwave pinged and Cate sank back onto the bar seat, unsure whether or not to be relieved or terrified. *God, that was close*, she thought. And the evening had hardly even begun.

CHAPTER 7

Carrying a bucket containing cloths and numerous polishes and sprays, Cate walked towards Nancy's bedroom feeling sick with fear and excitement. It was her first real spying assignment.

Just half an hour earlier, she had been up on the top deck serving champagne to a slightly drunk Nancy who was clinging to a rather bored-looking Tass.

Jules and Lulu stood to one side, pointedly ignoring the display of awkward affection. Cate even thought she saw contempt in Lulu's face as she watched Nancy planting kisses on the handsome Russian's cheek, but she could have been wrong.

The soft, early evening darkness had pushed back the last of the sun's rays and the splash pool, lit up by underwater lights, stood out against the twilight like a huge shimmering sapphire.

After such a hot day, the cool night-time air felt like a caress on Cate's bare arms as she handed out drinks to the four adults, none of whom bothered to thank her.

A table for two, laid with crisp white linen and furnished with silver cutlery and a double candelabra had been set by the side of the pool. As Marcus carried in a seafood paella and lobster platter, Lulu and Jules stood up.

'We're off to town,' announced Jules. 'We'll see you guys in the morning.'

Neither Tass nor Nancy took any notice of his words. Indeed they didn't even look in his direction but, as they left the deck, Lulu beckoned sharply to Cate to follow.

'Leave them,' she hissed as Cate moved up behind her. 'Can't you see they want to be alone?'

Cate followed behind, then watched carefully as Jules and Lulu tottered off down the pontoon. Cate began to account for everyone left on board. Tass and Nancy were safely on the top deck. Marcus was still in the galley: she could hear his singing as he concocted some amazing dessert, and Wendy was waiting on the main deck until whatever time the happy couple decided to call it a night.

Downstairs in the staff mess room, Cate found Bill playing cards with Mikey whilst Ahmed sat away from the others, on one of the red bar stools. It was a perfect time to go spying.

Cate made a big show of going over to the small sink and pulling out cleaning products and a bucket. 'Just tidying up some of the main rooms,' she said to no one in particular. Bill and Mikey ignored her and carried on with their good-natured banter but Ahmed turned and gave her a slow stare.

'Which rooms?' he asked.

'Not sure yet,' said Cate blithely. 'P'raps the main salon and the bathrooms. Depends.'

'Tell me when you're going into Miss Kyle's room,' Ahmed said, gazing into Cate's eyes as he spoke. She held his gaze but behind his pale eyes there was an emptiness which made Cate shudder inwardly. 'I like to check and double check. Understand?' He spoke flatly, without drama and Cate struggled to find a reply. Then Bill came to her rescue.

'Blimey, mate, you're a bit keen.' The Australian spoke without looking up from the cards he was holding.

'That's Ahmed for you,' said Mikey. 'Likes to keep 'imself busy.'

Cate nodded and went back upstairs clutching her bucket and dusters. She didn't have much time, she reckoned, before Ahmed came looking for her. Something told her he wasn't the type to make idle threats.

Cate hesitated, wondering whether to ask Marcus to act as look out, but when she poked her head around the galley door he was gone, the kitchen immaculate and clearly shut up for the night. Cate cursed silently, thought for a few seconds and then ran back downstairs. She nipped into her room, grabbed her laptop from under the bed and then went to the laundry cupboard and pulled down a couple of thick towels.

With the computer tucked between them, she carried the towels ostentatiously and slowly past the mess room door. Out of the corner of her eye she saw Ahmed look up as she went by. To him she was just carrying a pile of towels. He had no idea that they were hiding another pair of eyes.

At the top of the stairs, she dumped the towels, opened up

the laptop and removed the tiny detachable webcam. Looking quickly around her, she spotted a crack between the door and the wall and, switching the camera on, she slid it quickly into the gap.

Reaching the safety of the middle deck she heaved a huge sigh of relief. So far, so good. But she had very little time left to play with. She picked up the towels and laptop again and walked quickly towards Nancy's suite, then stopped and listened intently, her heart beating loudly, her breath shallow.

All was quiet, with just a few sounds of chat and music wafting down from the top deck where, pudding over, Nancy was presumably still snuggling up to her man. But just to make sure, she knocked softly on the door, then a second time more loudly. She opened it quietly. The bedroom was almost dark, lit only by a wavering light coming in through the portholes.

Cate padded silently over to the bedside table and switched on one of the lamps which gave out a light just bright enough to see by but, she hoped, dim enough not to attract attention. Nervously, she checked out the bathroom and the dressing room, looking behind the doors and back into the depths of the closets. To her relief there was no one lurking – she was definitely on her own.

She switched on the laptop, put it on the dressing table, clicked for the webcam viewer and held her breath. To her delight a flickering picture of the lower stairwell came up on the screen. She turned up the volume and within seconds could hear the faint noise of Bill and Mikey chatting just a few metres away. It was basic, she couldn't make out what they were saying, but it did the job. As long as Cate kept an eye and an ear out for her laptop, she should have advance warning of anyone who came up the stairs from below deck.

Now she was ready to go to work. She started in the bathroom, rummaging amongst the numerous bottles of Crème de la Mer cleanser, La Prairie night cream, and Bulgari scented body soufflés, valiantly resisting the urge to spray some extremely expensive Tom Ford Night Orchid on her wrists.

She moved on into the dressing room and worked her way methodically through the clothes in the wardrobe, checking even the smallest pockets and the linings, but the best she could come up with were receipts from Harvey Nichols (three sarongs), Gucci (two pairs of sunglasses) and Tiffany's (a gold ankle chain). She even checked inside and underneath each of the exquisite shoes.

For a few seconds she stopped and caught herself in the middle of her task. *How do I know how to do this?* she wondered. *Just how have I come from being a schoolgirl on the number 42 bus to a secret agent searching the shoes of a supermodel?*

The drawers were crammed with at least fifteen handbags that Cate had never seen before, ranging from tiny little Chanel evening numbers with delicate gold chains to a huge vintage Kelly bag that looked as if it belonged on a Sixties film set.

Despite her best intentions, Cate was starting to flag; the tension and the fear of being caught, not to mention the lack of anything specific to search for, was beginning to grind her down. As the seconds ticked by it was becoming harder and harder to fight the voice in her head that was saying, 'Get out! Get out now!'

But still she hesitated. She didn't, couldn't, just give up. Not when logic and instinct told her that somewhere in this room could be the information that could help her discover the dreadful fate of those lovely animals.

The flickering screen of the laptop showed that she had already got through four minutes of searching time and Cate, suddenly panicked that she might have missed some signal of approaching danger, used up a few more precious seconds standing by the speaker, ears straining to hear any unusual sound.

But there was no change, nothing to hear apart from the reassuring murmur of the men from the deck below and the music coming from the top deck. She forced herself to stop and think. If Nancy Kyle was carrying something precious, or dangerous, with her, she wouldn't want the hassle of finding a hiding place every time she checked in somewhere new. It was risky and inconvenient. Far better to keep it hidden in something that travelled with her, something familiar, and easy to reach.

But what? Cate had already checked Nancy's clothes and her toiletries and just about everything else in her suite that went where she did. Perhaps there was nothing to find. Maybe Marcus and his mates had got it all completely wrong about Nancy.

And just then, Cate's gaze fell onto the large silver-framed photograph of Nancy with the mountain gorilla and she nearly kicked herself with frustration at her stupidity. How could she have missed such an obvious hiding place?

Cate turned over the heavy frame and undid the catches at

the back. The thick wood backing came away easily and taped on the inside was a piece of paper. Cate let out a breath of air. Success.

Trying hard to control her natural inclination to rip away the tape, Cate instead carefully peeled it from the frame, noting exactly where it had been placed. The thick piece of paper was small, less than ten centimetres by fifteen centimetres and folded over twice. Curiously Cate opened it.

The beautiful and the rare animals of the wilderness thank you for your generosity and courage. Your name will go down in history. Such a beautiful woman, you are, quite literally, saving our planet.

Despite herself, Cate found herself grinning at the flowery language, before beginning the task of working out the flamboyant signature at the bottom. It took a few seconds to pick up the rhythm of the bright green inked letters but finally she had it. Frederico Mantoni. Or it could be Mantani. She had no idea of knowing whether it was important but at least it was something concrete to go on.

Quickly she reread and memorised the message and then replaced the letter. Luckily the tape still held and if it did come away the next time it was removed, Cate reasoned, it would look accidental. She replaced the frame exactly as it had been on the bedside table and went to check the other photographs. The first one, showing Nancy with a turtle, drew a blank. The next, a smaller one of her with a Siberian tiger, was empty as well. Cate had just checked the last frame when suddenly, through the speakers, she heard the sound she had been dreading. Footsteps, treading heavily up the staircase and headed her way. Not quickly, but Cate calculated that, even so, she had less than a minute to cover her tracks and get out of the room.

With no time to be frightened, her mind went into overdrive. The laptop was shut down and hidden within the pile of towels on the bed in seconds. Cate switched off the light and opened the door quietly, giving silent thanks for the thick pile carpet that silenced her footsteps. She grabbed the towels and the cleaning equipment and slipped quietly and quickly out of the room and across into a guest bedroom, shutting the door behind her. Like a whirlwind she ran into the bathroom, turned on the taps and raced back again to the door where she stood, breathless and listening.

Less than ten seconds passed before Cate heard the door to Nancy's room being opened and held her breath, waiting to see if she had left behind any evidence that would betray her to the bodyguard. But there was nothing, no explosion of anger, no shout of annoyance and at last Cate allowed herself to breathe easy. That had been close, very close. And she wasn't out of the woods just yet.

A minute later, when Ahmed barged unceremoniously into the second bedroom, he found Cate in the ensuite bathroom, humming a song and scrubbing the bath with faultless industry.

'Oh hi,' she said in a surprised voice to Ahmed as she turned to see him. 'Glad you're here. I've nearly finished up. Can we go and do Nancy's room now?'

An hour later, her cleaning finished and given the rest of the night off by a weary-looking Wendy, Cate was back in her cabin. Checking that her door was securely locked, she knelt on the floor, powered up her laptop, switched on the scrambler and went into Google. Frederico Mantoni drew a blank. So did Frederico Mantani. But Frederico Mantanini – Professor Frederico Mantanini to be precise – had over three million entries, almost all of them alluding to his controversial work in the field of human cloning.

Cate looked hard at his image – a strange-looking man with a beaky nose, and unusually, one brown and one blue eye. He looked clever, urbane, self-important even. But he didn't look wicked.

'Arthur,' said Cate to her younger brother who had, rather unwillingly, been roused from a game of *Star Wars Battleship* by a series of increasingly frequent pings from his sister. 'I think we have just made a breakthrough. Nancy has a thank-you letter from one of the few doctors in the world who will admit to experimenting with human cloning. In fact, two years ago, this Professor Mantanini claimed he was successful and had delivered a baby who was a clone of its long dead brother. But when he didn't produce this cloned baby for medical examination, he was laughed out of the public arena and even those who supported him dropped him like a bad smell. He was struck off the Italian medical register and stripped of his professorship from the University of Milan.

'He hasn't really been heard of since, although some say he is now working for a lab in Eastern Europe, where the regulations on genetic research are a bit more flexible than they were in Italy. Wherever he is, he has been in contact with Nancy Kyle, that's for sure.'

'And not to discuss human cloning,' Arthur echoed Cate's

thoughts. 'She already has more than enough babies for one person.'

'Nope,' said Cate flatly. 'Not for babies. Perhaps animals. Rare endangered animals. Just think of the kudos that would come your way if you managed to clone a mountain gorilla or giant panda, say. People have been working on cloning since Dolly the Sheep, but they aren't able to clone all animals, and anyway, nothing cloned has ever survived for long. If you could, though, you would save an entire species from oblivion. It would resurrect his career in an instant.'

'It's not just the kudos,' said Arthur slowly. 'Have you any idea how much he could charge for his expertise if he succeeded? But no one would let him anywhere near animals like that, not for experimental research.'

'Not him, sure,' agreed Cate. 'But an international supermodel with friends in high places and a well-known interest in animals might find it a bit easier. I don't want to believe it, but it seems as if the further I get into this, the more explaining Nancy has to do. I have to get to Marcus and tell him what I know.'

'Hold on,' said Arthur quickly. 'I've got some news to report as well. First of all, your gorgeous friend Tass. Guess what his boat – or rather his dad's boat – is called?' Arthur could hardly keep the triumph from out of his voice. 'Go on, try.'

'I give up!' said Cate with amused exasperation.

'Rubbish, sis,' laughed her brother. 'Seriously though, it made the hairs on the back of my neck stand up. His yacht is only called *The Good Times*.' He paused theatrically, waiting for the news to sink in, watching his sister's reaction. He was not disappointed. The colour drained from Cate's cheeks as her mind rushed back to those terrible moments only the day before when she had thought she was witnessing the death of a man.

'Tell the Roman to look for the good times,' Andrei had said to her.

And the good times was nothing to do with remembering the past. It was about a boat. A specific boat with links to Nancy Kyle.

Cate groaned inwardly. 'I just thought Andrei was rambling,' she said more to herself than Arthur. The Roman – of course, that was Marcus, a Latin name.

She thought for a minute then spoke again. 'Arthur, well done,' said Cate. 'I need to speak to Marcus immediately and I have to get onboard that yacht.'

'It won't be easy,' said Arthur, who had clearly done his homework thoroughly. 'According to the blueprints of the boat, which I just happened to find on the highly secure website of the New Zealand yacht builders who designed it, *The Good Times* is one of the most secure boats in the world. In fact, it is one of the top twenty most expensive boats ever built, mainly because of the security features it carries.

'Apparently Tass's father is the paranoid type – not surprising when you consider that he has already survived three attempts on his life. Probably because he made his money making dodgy gas deals in very dodgy countries.

'The entire hull is bullet and bomb proof, there is a NASA-designed sonar centre which can pick up a fish farting four miles away and it carries a full range of weapons – from rifles to anti-aircraft missiles. Not to mention twenty-four-hour CCTV cameras covering every centimetre of the boat, and a panic room equipped with enough oxygen and food to last for two weeks. There's also a helicopter landing pad – naturally – and the latest must-have toy, a submarine with a docking bay in the lower decks.'

'Wow,' said Cate. She couldn't think of what else to say.

'You won't get on board by stealth,' said Arthur. 'I doubt if even a small navy could do that.'

'Well,' said Cate, 'in that case it will just have to be by invitation.'

As if on cue, there was a loud knocking on her door. 'Cate, are you awake?' It was Bill, sounding harassed. 'Nancy wants to go ashore and find a party. And she wants us all to come with her to keep her company.'

An hour later, Nancy, Tass, Cate, Wendy and Bill, not to mention a grumpy-looking Mikey and a very sullen Ahmed, were arranged around a large oval table in the basement of one of the coolest restaurants in Antibes. Marcus, who was nowhere to be found on the boat, had been texted and was expected to arrive at any minute.

The room was dark with deep red walls and aged wooden floors. Black and white pictures of famous jazz singers hung over the long timber bar and young waiters, wearing classic Fifties black and white uniforms, carried large trays of drinks which they swooped and swung over the heads of the crowded tables. At the back of the room, crammed to one side of a small, badly lit dance floor, a jazz quintet ripped enthusiastically and efficiently through a series of Ella Fitzgerald, Miles Davis and Dave Brubeck classics.

The band, who had their audience mesmerised by their skill, were an eclectic mix: a very old grey-haired and bearded double bass player, a young Japanese female pianist who didn't once look up from the piano keys, a seriously good-looking black trumpeter, a skinny drummer with long blond hair who could have been either a man or a woman and a very young, dark-haired saxophonist who looked strangely familiar.

It was a heady atmosphere, a combination of lively and relaxed, and it was impossible not to get into the spirit of things. Nancy and Tass ordered drinks all round and then, after a few minutes of gazing into each other's eyes, suddenly got to their feet.

'Come on, dance, have fun,' shouted Tass to a table of bemused-looking French couples who were seated next to them.

Cate had forgotten how good it felt to dance. At one point, Nancy was her partner, then Wendy and Bill had a go at whirling her around the dance floor. To widespread cheers, Nancy climbed onto a table and began dancing and blowing kisses at the band.

Then Tass grabbed the microphone to sing along to a Louis Armstrong number in a surprisingly tuneful voice and Nancy came down from the table to join him at the microphone.

The band good-naturedly played up to them, keeping the number going until Tass and Nancy had tired of singing and gone back to their seats waving regally to the now cheering restaurant clientele. Then, suddenly the set was over, the lights were up and the musicians were setting down their instruments and thirstily gulping down glasses of water.

Cate sat back down and took a sip of her Diet Coke. As she did so she noticed, to her astonishment, that the saxophonist was headed straight for her.

'*Bonjour encore.*' He stood over her, his deep blue eyes looking amused at her obvious confusion. 'We met yesterday. I was playing volleyball and you were running along the beach?'

Of course, it was him, the boy who had asked her to join in the match at the yacht club. Tonight he looked older than he had in his shorts and T-shirt – perhaps eighteen or nineteen – but his face was friendly and gentle and there was no hint of the aggression Cate had seen in some boys who had tried to chat her up in the past.

She smiled in recognition and, taking this as an invitation, he dropped into the seat next to her. Out of the corner of her eye Cate could see Wendy and Nancy grinning like idiots at this latest development, but if the boy noticed he didn't seem to care.

'I'm Michel, Michel le Blanc,' he volunteered, holding out his hand for Cate to shake.

'I'm Cate Carlisle,' said Cate, still slightly shocked by the sudden turn of events.

'I like the way you dance, Cate Carlisle,' said Michel, still holding onto her hand.

'I like the way you play the saxophone.' Cate grinned, recovering fast.

'So we're equal,' said Michel, smiling back at her and suddenly the noise of the bar receded into the background. 'But I want to ask you a question.'

'Such as?' said Cate, teasing him.

'Such as why are you here, where are you from, can I buy you a drink tomorrow?'

'That's three questions,' said Cate, enjoying the banter. 'How about you tell me three things about yourself first then I'll answer your questions.'

Michel's blue eyes were dancing with delight. 'I can see you are hard work,' he said. 'But definitely worth it. OK. I am eighteen years old and Antibes is my hometown. I am a student but in the holidays I work for my father in his restaurant here in the town. Now, your turn.'

'I come from everywhere. I am working on a yacht, *Catwalk II*, here in the marina and Nancy is my boss. And yes, you can buy me a drink sometime. Will that do for now?'

'*Oui.*' He dropped a piece of paper on the table in front of her. 'I have to go now – we are playing in another bar tonight. But take my number, yes? And my father's café is Le Rousillon just off the main square. Come in and I'll be there. If not, ask for me at the bar and they'll tell you where I am. I hope you do. *Au revoir*, Cate Carlisle.'

He stood up and lifted his hand in a gesture of farewell. Then he was gone. Cate sat still for a moment, wondering if she had just dreamt the entire conversation, until Nancy brought her abruptly out of her thoughts.

'Wow, babe,' she purred. 'Have you got like a kind of aura about you that attracts the guys?'

Cate dissolved into laughter but Nancy stayed serious. 'Listen up, Cate,' she said, throwing a friendly arm around the younger girl's shoulders. 'Sax appeal equals sex appeal and that guy has got it in spades. If I were ten years younger . . . in fact, what does that matter? Look at Demi Moore. Put that number into your phone right now.'

Now Cate was blushing furiously and Wendy, seeing her embarrassment, kindly came to her rescue.

'Right, Cate, you're on the early shift tomorrow. I think you should get back to the boat and get some kip. Will you be OK on your own? I could get Ahmed or Mikey to walk you back.'

She stood up. 'Wendy, I'll be fine.'

Once outside the bar, the air was cool and fresh and, as the noise of the town faded behind her, Cate felt herself relaxing. The stars were out and a gentle breeze was coming in from beyond the harbour. Lights from fishing boats heading out on the tide trailed across the sea in front of her and she could hear snatches of conversations from the fishermen coming across the water as they prepared for their long night ahead.

Cate paused, running back over the events of the evening in her head and then, after a minute of agonising whether she should or shouldn't, texted Michel her number, crossing her fingers as it disappeared from her screen.

Suddenly she heard the soft sound of footsteps tracking closely behind her, but when she turned there was no one to be seen. She hadn't imagined it she was sure. Was she being followed again?

She increased her pace and headed straight for the packed marina car park. The dim lighting and rows of cars and motorbikes provided the perfect cover for her and within seconds she had dodged in and out of so many vehicles that she knew it would have been impossible for anyone without supernatural night vision to have kept track of where she was.

She paused for a minute, listening. Only the tinkling of yacht masts and snatches of music from the restaurants on the other side of the wall disturbed the night silence. Then she heard someone singing quietly and instantly knew just who had been shadowing her.

'Marcus,' Cate called out softly, 'if you want to talk to me why don't you call me on my mobile?'

'Very funny, Cate.' Suddenly Marcus was right beside her, his large frame as solid as a statue in the poorly lit car park. 'Actually, the mobile phone is a very unreliable and unsafe piece of equipment. It can give away your position and it is very easily tapped.'

'Thanks for the lecture.' Cate was worn out and tetchy. She wanted to go to bed and dream about Michel.

'Mmmm,' said Marcus, looking at her as if he couldn't understand why she wasn't hanging onto his every word. 'OK. I just wanted an update, to find out if you had learnt anything new today.'

Cate shrugged. Where to begin? Quietly and methodically she worked her way through the events of the afternoon, telling him what she had found in Nancy's room, about the professor, what Andrei had said, and finally what Arthur had discovered about *The Good Times*. When she had finished Marcus let out a quiet whistle and pulled out his phone to make a call.

'Cate, I knew you were good but, man, you are really good,' he said in a low voice. 'I was right; you're just perfect for this job. I would never have been able to get into that bedroom without setting off very loud alarm bells in those bodyguards' sharp little brains and it was damn clever of you to think of looking in the picture frames.' He beamed proudly. 'And that brother of yours. It's like we got two for the price of one. Tell him from me, he's one cool dude.'

Just then Cate felt her mobile phone vibrating in her pocket and felt herself blushing. Could it be Michel calling her so soon?

She tried to ignore her disappointment when she realised it was Wendy. 'Just to warn you, Cate, you'd better get some beauty sleep. Nancy has decided we're all off to St Tropez in the morning.'

CHAPTER 8

Cate woke early to an unfamiliar but overwhelming sound. It was coming from beneath and around her cabin, a throbbing rhythm that reminded her of being in the mosh pit at a rock gig.

It took her a few seconds to work out that the massive engines that powered *Catwalk II* were up and running, all four of them producing an energy which could only be described as awesome. Cate looked quickly out of her porthole. *Catwalk II* was still moored up in her usual spot in the marina.

Bill must be giving the engines a warm up before we go out, thought Cate, enjoying the sense of anticipation uncoiling in her stomach.

She had a shower, washed and dried her hair and then tied it up in a ponytail. Up on deck, Bill was sitting at the steering console, watching the weather report on his sat nav. As Cate came towards him, he flicked the master switch to shut down the engines and slowly, almost painfully, they fell silent.

'Morning,' said Cate. 'Everything ready for the trip?'

'Uh huh.' Bill was clearly not a morning person. 'Right, Cate, you'd better get up on top deck and start storing all the movables away. Bring the sun loungers down below, shut up the bar and put away the parasols. We're not a huge boat and, although the weather forecast is showing calm, you can never be sure. Once we get past the point and head out to the main channel the wind can change really quickly.'

Cate nodded. Once they left the marina, *Catwalk II* was no longer a floating luxury hotel but a proper boat which had to obey the laws of the sea. She helped herself to a bottle of ice-cold water from the fridge in the salon and set to work.

At around eight, Marcus made an appearance in the galley and began to cook breakfast. Pretty soon the irresistible smell of frying bacon wafted out to the decks and Cate suddenly realised that she was ravenous. Ten minutes later, she and Bill sat cross-legged on the top deck in companionable silence, munching their way through a huge fried breakfast, all washed down with a large mug of tea.

Through the railings, Cate could see shoals of tiny silvery fish darting in and out of mooring ropes and knobbly brown strands of seaweed. The sky was already a deep unbroken blue and the dew that had formed overnight had burned off from even the shaded areas of the deck.

'It's going to be a hot one,' said Bill, putting his plate to one side.

Bill smiled at her and suddenly Cate felt a surge of contentment. Yesterday's events seemed like a dream, as if they had happened to another person.

Wendy came on deck, clutching a mug of coffee. 'Great dancing last night, Bill,' she grinned wickedly. 'Amazing shapes. But did you have to tread on *all* my toes?'

'Typical Yarpie, always blaming someone else for their misfortune,' said Bill good-humouredly. 'It's just the same with cricket.'

Wendy rolled her eyes at Cate who grinned at them both. Bill and Wendy were such a good match, she thought, but of course neither of them realised it. Maybe one day.

At ten a.m. precisely, with no sign of life from Nancy, Jules or Lulu, Bill fired up the engines once more, and with immaculate precision the huge boat began to edge out of its mooring.

It was an agonisingly slow process and it had to be. Six million pounds' worth of yacht, with another six million moored on either side, meant that one false move, one tiny scratch or dent, could cost the insurers a small fortune and probably Bill his job. But Bill knew what he was doing and soon the boat had safely left her neighbours and was nosing away from the ancient harbour and out to sea.

Cate was just texting Arthur their code when she heard a voice close by. 'Look behind you.' Marcus had come to join her up on the bow, a white baseball cap tipped over his eyes and a mug of tea in his hand.

'Cate, I've passed on to Henri all the information you discovered yesterday. Let's just say that what you told us has helped us to fit together a few more pieces of the puzzle.' Marcus was speaking quietly and urgently.

'There's more. The group we had under surveillance – the

thugs who put Andrei in a coma – chartered a helicopter first thing this morning. And guess what?' He didn't wait for an answer but continued grim-faced. 'That same helicopter landed in a hotel garden in St Tropez just over thirty minutes ago. Make no mistake, we aren't headed to St Tropez purely for pleasure. Someone on the *Catwalk II* has a spot of business to do as well. The question is, who?'

'Nancy,' said Cate immediately. 'It's her boat and she calls the shots.'

'She's the obvious one,' agreed Marcus. 'But let's keep an open mind. Anyone could have put the idea into her head last night. Anyone.'

'You want me to find out who.' It was a statement from Cate, not a question.

'Thanks, Cate.' Marcus sounded relieved. 'I know you've done so much already but you're just not going to arouse suspicion in the way I will. And let's face it – you're a natural.'

Cate cringed and pulled a face. She loathed being buttered up.

'OK, OK,' said Marcus, reading her expression with uncanny accuracy. 'Well, you *are* a natural, but let's be honest, I want you to do a job for me that I just can't do.'

'That's better,' said Cate, grinning.

'I'm stuck on the boat preparing food for tomorrow. Nancy and Tass have got a stack of friends coming on board for the day. But with any luck, you'll be free to go ashore once we've arrived,' Marcus carried on in a low voice. 'If I get a chance, I'll get back and search her room again. You must try to keep an eye on who wants to rush off the boat and find out where they're headed. Don't discount anyone, but keep an especially close eye on Nancy.'

Marcus's tone suddenly changed. 'Next time, if you want a cup of tea you'll have to come and get it yourself,' Marcus said, laughing. 'Worth coming up here for the view.' He nodded to Bill who had suddenly appeared just a few metres away from Cate. How long had he been standing there?

Cate suddenly laughed to herself. Bill spying on them? Lovely Aussie Bill, working for the bad guys? Not likely. She was getting paranoid.

Two hours later, with Nancy still showing no sign of emerging from her suite, the rumble from the engines slowed and quietened. *Catwalk II* was heading into St Tropez harbour.

Cate had heard and read so much about this beautiful French port – had even seen photographs and paintings – but nothing could have prepared her for her first sight of the town in real life.

Unlike Antibes, there was no fort perched high on a hill, no grim stone walls, not even an enclosed marina to block the view. Instead, the curved harbour came to meet the open sea, revealing pastel pink, green and beige buildings that stood red-tiled against a searing blue sky.

Then, as *Catwalk II* edged closer, Cate could see the prows of the gleaming yachts that were crammed, rear end first, into every centimetre along the wooden-fronted harbour.

Between the yachts and the tall, elegant buildings which huddled together around the open harbour, lay the cobbled quayside, where restaurants and bars spilled out almost down to the water's edge. Soft top sports cars – Bentleys, Lamborghinis and the odd, lowly Porsche – were parked, presumably whilst their owners enjoyed a few hours wandering between the cafés and the shops.

Just as Cate was wondering if Nancy would ever emerge to enjoy the sights, she made her entrance into the salon.

As usual, Nancy looked amazing. Her lime and orange summer dress was cut on the bias and flounced out from the bodice into a tulip skirt. The matching head band with tails drifting down her back would have looked ridiculous on anyone else, but on Nancy, with her height and figure, she simply looked as if she had stepped out of a Sixties film.

Only the diamond-studded phone clamped to her ear spoilt the illusion, not helped by the fact that she was barking down it in her all too familiar Essex accent.

'Pierre, you are a god . . . no, you are a god.' Nancy was clearly in full charm mode. 'We'll be with you by one, I promise, promise, promise, promise and can I please, please, please, darling, have that table under the big tree right by the beach. You know the one.' There was silence. 'Pierre, darling, I love that table, you know I do.' There was another silence. 'Franc who? What movie? God, that was years ago. I wasn't even born then. Can't you move them? Tell him I'll buy him champagne, give him an autograph, a kiss, whatever.' There was a pause, then Nancy played her final card. 'Tass is meeting me there and you know how he loves that table.' Another silence and then a scream of delight. 'Pierre, I adore you more than my mother, I swear it. Half an hour and we'll be moored up. I can't wait to give you the biggest kiss ever.' Nancy shut her phone, heaved a sigh of relief and threw her arms around the nearest person, who happened to be an astonished Cate. 'We're in!' she said. 'That Pierre, he never can resist me.'

'Le Ricochet?' Lulu asked Nancy.

Nancy nodded, her eyes shining.

Half an hour later, the boat was out of the harbour and rounding the coastline into Pampelonne Beach. One hundred metres out from land, the sea resembled a massive floating parking lot as at least thirty large yachts, many of them dwarfing *Catwalk II*, jostled for room to drop an anchor.

Most of them had helipads, all carried jet skis and had speed boats moored up alongside them. As they sailed slowly alongside one particularly huge yacht, Cate spotted two men on the top deck playing tennis on what looked like a full-sized court. She shook her head. This really was beyond awesome.

Suddenly the *Catwalk II* engines slammed into reverse thrust, the boat slowed gradually to a standstill and then Cate heard a rattle from far beneath her as the ten tonne anchor plummeted on its hefty chain down onto the sea bed below them.

With the engines cut for the first time in three hours, there was an overwhelming sense of peace and silence, broken only by the sound of waves splashing gently onto the hull of the boat and the hum of chat and laughter coming from the shoreline.

Cate saw a small, deep lilac speedboat, nosing its way out from the beach pontoon towards the *Catwalk II*. Pierre had obviously been keeping an eye out for them. Nancy appeared on the middle deck, applying last-minute lipstick and smelling of expensive perfume, trailed by Jules and Lulu who were both dressed in white linen, so bright that it hurt Cate's eyes just to look at them.

'Cate, you're coming with us,' Nancy said, much to Cate's surprise. 'I want a lovely, big table full of happy, smiling people.' She stuck her head through into the inner deck where Bill was now chatting and joking with Wendy. 'You too, guys,' she said.

'OK,' said Bill, coming back outside, 'but I'll take our own boat just in case there are any problems and I have to come back to *Catwalk II* quickly. I'll follow you to the restaurant.'

'Yeah, whatever.' Nancy wasn't interested in the details.

Lulu, standing behind her, turned to Cate and looked her up and down. 'You look like a cleaning lady,' she said with her usual charm. 'I wouldn't expect you to know it, but Le Ricochet happens to be one of the most exclusive restaurants in the entire world. People wait for months just to get a table. You've got two minutes to go and make yourself look respectable.'

Bullying always made Cate want to fight back and this time was no exception. She would show Lulu. Back in her cabin she leapt into the shower for thirty seconds to freshen up then, whilst she dried, opened her tiny wardrobe, scanned it and quickly settled on a pair of lemon capri pants and her one expensive top, a short asymmetrical Jil Sander kaftan that Monique had passed on to her.

She quickly undid her ponytail and stuck her head upside down to brush out her thick blond hair. She just had time for a quick flick of mascara, a slick of her favourite pink lip-gloss and a squirt of perfume and to grab her rucksack, then she was running back up to the deck just as the tender from Le

Ricochet came alongside the *Catwalk II*.

'You look lovely, Cate,' said Wendy, cool and elegant in a three-quarter-length baby blue kaftan.

'Sure does,' said Marcus, who had just appeared. Even Nancy gave her an appreciative nod, although predictably Lulu shot her a filthy look.

Who cares? thought Cate. *I'm getting used to your little ways and they don't bother me any more, you miserable old bag.* She giggled to herself as the small group, headed by Nancy, stepped one by one from the rear of the large yacht into the little boat.

'Welcome aboard.' The boatman seemed genuinely delighted to see them, greeting them with smiles and hand kisses as they boarded his vessel.

As she looked over towards the fast approaching beach, Cate shivered, part in excitement and part in fear. She had crossed a boundary now, from interested bystander to a player in an increasingly sinister investigation. The next few hours could see her world changed forever.

CHAPTER 9

Clearly Nancy could hardly contain her excitement, craning her neck and even jumping up from her seat to try to get a better view ahead. Finally, she could bear it no longer.

'Will Pierre be there to meet me?' she asked the boatman. 'Does he know I'm here?'

Cate cringed with embarrassment, but either the boatman had impeccable manners, or he had heard it all a thousand times before. 'Madame Nancy,' he said smoothly, 'Pierre is beside himself with excitement at your coming. It is an honour. See, here he is on the pontoon.'

Cate looked at a tall, middle-aged man who was standing on the wooden jetty which was now just metres away from them. His thick, dark hair was turning grey, but his body looked fit and toned and even from this distance you could see he had an air of supreme confidence. This was a man in charge of his kingdom.

He stood still until the tender came alongside and then strode over to extend a hand to Nancy as she jumped, dangerously quickly, from the boat onto the pontoon.

'Darling Pierre,' she shrieked, throwing her arms around his neck and depositing lipstick kisses all over his tanned face. 'It's been too long. You're looking so gorgeous, there should be a law against it. I am just so, so, so, so excited to see you.'

Cate watched in admiration as, with precise charm and politeness, Pierre allowed himself to be embraced for just the right length of time before extracting himself gently and without causing any offence.

'Welcome to you all,' he said. 'Welcome to Le Ricochet. Your table is waiting.' And with that, the group was whisked onto the hot beach, up past the sunbathing customers and through a low wooden gate into the restaurant garden.

The place was breathtaking in its simplicity. Tables, some for two, some for twenty, all covered in pure white and deep blue tablecloths were dotted around underneath olive and eucalyptus trees. Each of the tables was set, immaculate glassware shining and silver cutlery gleaming. Above the tables, fairy lights were strung from the trees and, in the far corner of the garden, a woman was playing gentle jazz on the piano. It was utterly perfect and Cate, who had seen some fabulous places in her time, thought she had never been anywhere so beautiful in her life.

Many of the tables were already filling up with wealthy middle-aged couples, large beautifully turned-out family groups and, of course, those who were clearly in the throes of romance. As Cate looked around, she suddenly got the extraordinary sensation that she knew many of the lunch guests. She corrected herself hastily. She didn't actually know them. It was just that she had seen them so many times, on TV and in newspapers and magazines, that they felt as familiar to her as her own family.

The first celebrity she spotted was a very leathery, very lecherous former Italian Prime Minister. True to form he was surrounded by a gaggle of nubile girls not much older than Cate, one of whom was feeding him a strawberry.

Over in the far corner sat a well-known golfer with his teenage sons and latest wife being entertained by a very lively BBC sports commentator who was clearly doing most of the talking. Across from him a former British cabinet minister only had eyes for a young Hollywood actress who was laughing uproariously at all his jokes. Cate passed by a larger table and realised it held six members of the past and present England football team. They were drinking sparkling mineral water, playing on their PSPs and somehow finding them more exciting than the persistent attentions of a group of stunning French girls who were giggling on the table next to them.

If she was impressed by her fellow celebrities, Nancy wasn't about to show it. In any case, she had an entrance to make. Following Pierre to her table, she sailed through the garden, pushing out her chest and wiggling her hips as she went, now and again stopping to give someone she knew a wave, or if they were really lucky, a kiss. PSPs were dropped, and even the aged Italian lothario suddenly ignored the pouting beauties at his table.

Pierre led them to what was undoubtedly the best table in the restaurant. Set right by the low fence that separated the beach from the garden, it was shaded by a gently rustling orange tree and had a spectacular view out over the bay and to the boats beyond.

Waiting for them was Tass, who, as Nancy strutted towards him, was looking rather like the cat who had got the cream. A very hungry-looking Mikey was chewing glumly on breadsticks and Ahmed was as morose as ever.

'Good table, Nancy,' said Tass, as she sashayed into the seat next to him and leant over for a long lingering kiss before helping herself to the stuffed olives on his plate. 'But do we really need to be joined by your entire staff?'

'Oh, darling,' said Nancy, sounding not at all put out. 'If you want this table you have to have a large group. Everyone knows that. Pierre won't put a table for two here, not even for me.' She smiled brightly around the table. 'Wendy, you order, babe. Fish, pasta, whatever.'

Cate was sure that she saw Pierre wince. 'Nancy,' he said suavely. 'I must go and oversee the kitchen. I'll send Jacques over to you and I'll be back to see you in an instant.'

The group devoured the antipasti, which was followed by the catch of the day – a huge plate of salt-encrusted roasted snapper set in a small sea of sparkling prawns – followed by fresh paw paws, mango, strawberries and blueberries with a delicate vanilla and Cointreau flavoured cream.

The feast finally over, the group began a hot debate on whether or not to move to the sun loungers on the beach.

'You guys make up your minds,' said Bill, getting up from the table. 'In the meantime, I've got some errands to do in the town – bits for the engines, that sort of thing. I'll love ya and leave ya.' And with that, he strode off.

Cate tried to look casual but inside her heart was racing. Was anyone else going to make their excuses and leave? Was Bill really off on an innocent errand, or was he up to something more sinister? She looked around the table. Nancy, Tass and Wendy, followed by the two bodyguards, were already starting to make their way down to the beach to settle on the sun loungers. Clearly they weren't going anywhere else anytime soon. And Lulu? Cate watched as she moved to a small chair in the shade of a tree, took out a book from her handbag and started reading. It looked like she too had little intention of moving for the rest of the afternoon, or was that just for show? But just as Marcus had suggested might happen, someone was leaving the group. And that someone was Bill. She had to make a decision fast.

'I've never been to St Tropez before,' said Cate. 'I think I might pop off and explore a little if that's OK.'

Wendy nodded vaguely at her over her shoulder but no one else in the party seemed to care either way.

Mentally crossing her fingers that she had picked the right option, Cate walked casually through the garden and then increased her pace once she was out of sight of the tables. She hoped she hadn't left it too long, that she hadn't already lost Bill before she had even started following him. To her relief, as she came out onto a quiet residential street, she saw him in the distance.

'I'm getting used to this,' said Cate grimly to herself, as she first checked behind her to see that no one else was following either her or Bill.

Bill showed no sign of being uneasy or nervous. He walked purposefully but without rushing, and Cate started to think she should have been keeping an eye on someone else.

But still she stuck to Bill, tracking him down the long street, which was edged with high houses all shuttered up against the bright afternoon sun, and then out onto a main road.

To her left she could see the harbour, glimpses of the bright blue sea visible through the numerous small parks and trees. But rather than head for the harbour and the shops, Bill took a right fork and began to walk briskly and purposefully up the hill and away from the town centre. It was harder now to keep him in her sights; the cars, motorbikes and pedestrians that thronged the busy tarmac road were obscuring her view and the cafés spilling out onto the pavements created a natural obstacle course. Cate had to jog to avoid losing him.

There was probably an innocent explanation, thought Cate to herself. Most likely he was heading for some kind of engineering workshop. The commercial road gradually faded away to be replaced by a shabby street with boarded-up offices and locked-up graffitied garages and then, suddenly, Bill stopped, outside a nondescript prefab building with painted panels that had the air of a small abandoned school.

Cate darted to the opposite side of the road and pressed herself into a small alleyway that ran between two old garages. The air was baking hot and chokingly dusty. Cate caught the whiff of stale oil and, as she looked behind her, she could see the alley was littered with old engine parts. That was it – he must be searching out an obscure engine part.

Bill knocked on a door that was set into a grubby white wall surrounding the property and, within seconds, it was opened by a man who stepped out into the street to shake his hand. Cate did a double take, hardly believing her eyes. There was no mistake, no forgetting that long lank hair. Standing just a few metres away from her, being greeted by Bill, was one of the men who had beaten Andrei half to death. She strained her ears to hear what they were saying and her heart sank. They were talking in Russian, both men chatting like natives.

'I can only speak Australian.' She remembered Bill standing in front of her on her very first day aboard *Catwalk II*, his face open and honest. The best type of liar. Could Bill really be one of the bad guys? It seemed almost beyond belief.

Suddenly a thought struck her. Perhaps Bill was investigating Nancy, too, either working for Marcus, like her, or even on his own. Cate knew she might well be clutching at straws but despite herself her spirits rose. She would watch and wait, and not jump to any conclusions.

The gate was propped open now, the lank-haired man leaning against it while Bill went inside. Five minutes, ten minutes passed while Cate grew increasingly anxious. Something wasn't right, she could sense it. The lank-haired man was nervy, chain-smoking, looking up and down the street and at the deserted buildings around him as if he feared he was being watched. At one point he turned and started to walk back into the building but then changed his mind and came out and resumed his manic pacing. Then he disappeared around the corner of the house and came back, pushing a large moped.

Even from her hiding place, Cate could sense his fear and now she was frightened too. She was sure something evil was about to happen, and she knew with certainty that she couldn't stop it. Suddenly there was a loud, muffled bang and the lank-haired man jerked his head almost involuntarily towards the house. A few minutes later Bill appeared, carrying a bright blue laptop under his arm, and nodded at his companion. Wordlessly, the lank-haired man gunned the moped. Bill pulled the gate shut behind him with a slam, secured it with a thick chain and padlock, and still clutching the laptop, hopped on behind him.

The dark blue machine was U-turning in the street, passing Cate at speed as it headed towards town. She watched as the bike disappeared in a cloud of dust. She could never hope to follow them and, for a few seconds, she felt like screaming and stamping in frustration.

She didn't allow herself to rant for long. That wasn't going to achieve anything. It was time to do a bit of exploring but first she needed a weapon and she wished for a second she had brought the gun. She eyed up the rubbish littering the ground behind her and spotted a thick metal pipe half hidden in the stringy grass. She pulled it out gratefully, dislodging two very surprised lizards as she did so, and gripped it tightly. It was perfect – just the right weight for her to carry, but heavy enough to inflict damage if necessary.

She watched the house across the road for a full five minutes. It seemed silent and empty, there was no movement from behind the boarded-up windows. She scanned the eaves and the roof but couldn't see any cameras.

Finally, plucking up the courage to move, Cate checked

that the road was clear, and, her hands slippery with nervous sweat, left the alleyway and crossed the road to the gate. The metal pipe made quick work of the padlock and Cate was through the gate and into the relative safety of the doorway. She paused for a breather and to try to still her nerves, listening to see if anyone had heard her, but there was complete silence. *Even the birds don't sing here,* thought Cate, and shuddered slightly.

She looked closely at the door, trying to size up what was keeping it shut. There was no visible lock, no obvious means of opening it up. She brought out the tiny tin that Marcus had given her. He had been thorough as he went through the list of equipment in the tin: 'An electromagnet for causing mayhem with computers, a tiny laser which will cut through metal, a data stick – with data card reader and a spare data card – with enough capacity to copy a NASA hard drive.'

She picked out the small hyper magnet. As she flicked the switch she felt the power surge through the tiny piece of metal, and it was all she could do to hang onto it before it escaped from her grasp. She placed it quietly on the door and slid it methodically from side to side, trying to work out where the lock was. Almost instantly it fixed onto the centre of the door where it clung like a limpet.

Gotcha, thought Cate triumphantly. She turned the tiny dial on the top of the magnet up to its highest setting. If the lock on the other side was controlled by any form of digital software, the magnet would scramble it and make it useless.

The gadget didn't let her down. Cate pushed gently on the door and it opened without protest into a dark, dingy corridor containing a staircase and not much else.

Clutching her weapon, she moved silently up the small, bare staircase. She reached the landing and paused, listening again, but there was nothing.

At the end of the landing, by a small boarded-up window which would once have looked out onto the street, stood a stained door which was covered with filth of every description, including something which looked horribly like blood. Cate noted two parallel gouges running down the side of the door. Were they claw marks? Something or someone had put up a good fight for their freedom.

Cate pushed at the old door. It wasn't locked. She found herself in a long room, the only light coming from a few chinks in the boarded-up windows. On the opposite wall stood barred cages stacked floor to ceiling, some large enough for a man, others not much bigger than a shoe box. The animals had obviously been kept here. No wonder the gang had chosen this virtually deserted district to house the animals. Even if anyone did hear them, it looked exactly the type of area where everyone minded their own business anyway.

Cate began methodically checking each of the cages, but they were empty, cleared out. Whatever creatures had been confined here had been moved elsewhere and Cate felt a hopelessness overwhelm her.

She took out her phone, and began taking pictures of the room, of the cages and the boarded windows. As she did so, she realised that there was a door at the far end of the room. Cate cursed herself for not being smart enough to check her surroundings before she started searching the cages. Anyone could be behind that door. She had put herself at risk and was lucky that so far she hadn't had to pay the price for her carelessness.

She was frightened now, her breathing coming in short shallow gasps. For a second, she considered fleeing back to the restaurant, but she knew that she had to keep trying to track down those poor, trapped animals.

As she reached the door, she had a sudden vision of Bill coming out of the house carrying the laptop with the air of a man who had just finished a job. She remembered the dull thump, the lank-haired man's frantic nervousness and the way both men had clearly been desperate to get away from the house.

Cate gently opened the door. This room was brightly lit, a stainless steel and white model of pristine cleanliness. Suddenly Cate knew exactly what she was going to find and for a minute her courage nearly failed her.

Everything was immaculate, like the science lab at Cate's school only bigger and better. Microscopes were lined up neatly on the metal worktops next to petri dishes and piles of needles and spatulas still wrapped in their plastic packaging. Clearly no expense had been spared. There were centrifugal machines and ovens, blood-washing machines and numerous fridges with thermometers that measured in fractions of degrees.

A dark-haired man was sitting behind a desk at the far end of the room. His deep set eyes, one brown, one blue, seemed to watch Cate as she went towards him, but he didn't move. Down the left side of his distinctive beak-like nose a small trickle of blood was already coagulating, but enough had spilled down to form a pool of darkness which was still spreading over his white-coated arm and onto the floor below.

As she walked determinedly towards him, Cate had the strangest feeing that he was desperately trying to say something to her, that he was not yet gone from this world. But even if he had wanted to talk, it was clear that, as Cate touched his still-warm hand, it was all too late for that. Professor Mantanini had been silenced forever.

CHAPTER 10

Looking back on it later, Cate was amazed that she didn't scream. Instead, almost on autopilot, she began taking more pictures, walking steadily and carefully around the body, making sure that she covered every angle. 'Sorry,' she found herself murmuring to the dead man, feeling guilty that she was invading his privacy. 'Sorry,' she muttered again as she almost tripped over an outstretched foot.

She had no idea why she was so calm. Although she had seen plenty of dead bodies on TV and in films and a few on the roads driving through a war zone in a UN convoy, this was different. Perhaps it was because he was only just dead. Perhaps because she was the first person to find him after he had died. She had heard the sound of the shot as he was murdered and now she felt attached to him, responsible for him even. She knew she would be haunted by the sight of him forever.

Cate was just about to call Marcus and tell him what she had found, when she smelt the first wafts of something sickly and sinister. She stopped what she was doing and sniffed the air, trying to work out what it was. The smell hit her like a wave, making her head spin. It was getting stronger, and now she could hear a low, hissing sound behind her. *Gas*, she thought with a gut-wrenching lurch of terror. *The room is filling with gas.*

She looked around frantically, following the sound, and spotted a tiny pipe that had been wrenched away from the wall behind the professor's desk. Hidden by a small shelf, Cate guessed that it had been slowly spewing its invisible poison into the air since Bill had left the house. Next to the pipe stood a small metal box on which a digital countdown spiralled towards zero. Cate had heard of this set-up before. In approximately four minutes it would trigger a spark to ignite the gas creating an explosion so huge it would no doubt obliterate the entire building.

The ultimate clean-up job, she thought grimly. *To blow the whole place to kingdom come and hope that no one would ever find the body. Or if they did, it would be pretty much impossible to identify.*

Her first reaction was to preserve the evidence of the horror in the room, and to do that she had to at least try to disarm the bomb. She reached for the magnet, sliding the lid off the survival kit with a shaking finger. Then she paused, suddenly cold with fear. What if the magnet sent the countdown haywire instead of stopping it, and tripped the device while she was standing over it?

By now she was feeling nauseous, her legs wobbly and weak, her mind a hazy mush of thoughts and emotions but she knew that now, more than ever, she needed to concentrate. There was certainly no point in freaking out or screaming for help. The only person who could keep her alive was herself. She had to get out of there!

She started to run, but her knees buckled beneath her after just a few metres. Gasping for breath, she crawled on her knees towards the door, her hands scrabbling desperately on the tiled floor for grip to pull her along. But any progress she made was agonisingly slow, it took at least a minute to make it to the first doorway and Cate knew that at this rate she had no chance of getting out of the building before the bomb went off.

With tears streaming down her face, she tried to pull her phone from her pocket. It was too late to call for help, she knew that, but she wanted to hear Arthur's voice to tell him that she loved him and to say goodbye. But, as she did so, her hand banged against the survival tin and she forced her mind back to the instructions Marcus had given her.

She could see him now, handing over the tin and shaking hands with her solemnly, finalising her agreement that she would do as he asked and spy on Nancy.

What on earth had she been thinking? That she, Cate Carlisle, a sixteen-year-old who had spent most of the last year revising for her GSCEs, could outwit experienced hardened criminals, men who thought nothing of assassinating witnesses and planting bombs? Was she now in danger of breaking the record for being the shortest-lived agent in the entire history of spying?

As she sprawled exhausted on the cold floor, Cate was laughing and crying at the same time, tears rolling down her cheeks. *It must be the gas*, thought Cate, making another huge effort to force herself to focus through the mental fog that was now threatening to overwhelm her.

Try to remember. There had been something that Marcus had laughed about when he showed her how it worked. 'This one's for fun,' he had said. 'This one is real secret agent stuff. And I promise that at the end of the summer you get to keep it as a souvenir.'

Of course, Cate thought, as she remembered the package she'd also been given. *The projectile pulley*. She nearly laughed out loud again as she pulled it out of her bag. At least before she died she would get to use a real-life spy gadget.

She fumbled clumsily in the semi-darkness and found the tiny fibreglass grip, aimed it at one of the chinks in the window boards and pressed the black firing button. The hook, with a thin wire attached to it, shot out with a power so strong that her arm was wrenched forward, causing a sharp pain to shoot through her shoulder focusing her mind and lifting the fug slightly. Cate held her breath and squinted at the window, but then her heart sank – she had missed her target, the hook had fallen short of the window and was lying uselessly on the floor.

Grunting with effort, she pressed the green button. The pulley self-wound, bringing the hook back with it and Cate, using her left hand to hold her trembling right one steady, fired again. This time she saw the hook disappear through the chink in the boards and smash the window. She tugged on it desperately and felt it come back on itself, holding fast against the boards.

She pulled harder in a final test, then, uttering a silent prayer that the hook would hold her weight, grabbed tightly with both hands, pressed the green button and in an instant was dragged at speed across the floor of the room towards the window. She removed the boards and pushed up the broken sash, gratefully gulping lungs full of fresh air.

Outside the sun was still blazing and the sky a bright blue, the tattered buildings opposite sharp in the sunlight. But she was still ten metres above the street with only seconds to go before the bomb exploded. Desperately she swung her legs out onto the sill and looked down to the concrete paving below. Her heart sank. There was nothing beneath her to cushion her fall and if she broke a leg or an ankle she would be left there like a wounded animal, unable to run for cover from the explosion. Then she remembered the pulley. She grabbed the hook and passed it back through the window, scrabbling around until it caught on the sill. 'I'm out of time,' she told herself. 'It's now or never.'

Holding the pulley tight, she said a quick prayer, pressed the black button and jumped. The pulley whizzed out above her and then, with a jerk, stopped dead, leaving Cate hanging just a metre above the ground. The relief that she wasn't plastered all over the concrete gave her a sudden burst of power. Kicking off from the wall, she jumped over the fence letting go of the wire and rolling as she hit the ground. She sprinted across the road, reaching the cover of the alleyway just as the building blew up into the clear blue sky.

Cate hadn't expected the noise. It was so loud that for a few seconds it deafened her, leaving her head ringing with pain.

Instinctively, she ducked as a fireball rolled along the street, followed by a cloud of debris which blotted out the sun and left her choking and gasping for breath. But she was alive. *Alive.* Even the ash that was falling in thick layers on her skin felt wonderful – proof that she had, against all the odds, survived.

Then there was silence. Cate wasn't quite sure what she had expected. Shouts maybe, frightened neighbours running out into the street, sirens wailing. But there was nothing, except a few dogs barking in the distance and the gentle breeze rustling in the trees.

She looked down and groaned. Her clothes were blackened and ripped, her legs and stomach covered in grazes from where she had clambered through the window and rolled across the concrete ground. People would take one look at her and call either an ambulance or the men in white coats or probably both. She could call Marcus but it would be too long before he got help to her.

Five minutes later, via back alleys and several brick walls, Cate had arrived at the first of the shopping streets. Most of the shops were shut for the siesta, but Cate spotted one still open, racks of clothes standing outside fluttering in the summer breeze.

She darted across the road and grabbed a lightweight cotton dress that looked approximately her size. Then she went into the shop and headed straight for the changing room at the back before the elderly shopkeeper had even registered her presence. As she pulled the curtain across she finally heard sirens – several of them by the sound of it.

She pulled her clothes off her bruised body, wincing as she

did so. The dress fitted pretty much perfectly, but as Cate looked at herself in the mirror, she grimaced at the grubby-faced girl staring back at her. Frantically she pulled her dirty hair back into a ponytail and wiped her face with what was left of her trousers before reaching into her rucksack and taking out some euros.

'*Pardon, mademoiselle.*' The old lady was outside the changing room now, sounding puzzled.

Cate pulled back the curtain suddenly, shoved the euros at the surprised lady, muttered an apology and was gone. She knew she had given her enough money to cover the cost of the new outfit and she had to hope that, if anyone came asking questions about the explosions, the old lady wouldn't put two and two together.

Ten minutes later, her dirty clothes dumped in a roadside bin, Cate slipped back into the garden of Le Ricochet, where everything seemed almost exactly as she had left it an hour or so before. Nancy and Tass were on the beach, surrounded by a host of glamorous-looking new-found friends. Wendy and Lulu were walking barefoot along the water's edge, with Jules trailing behind them. There was no sign of Bill or the *Catwalk II* tender. Presumably he had gone back to the boat on his own.

Cate sat cross-legged on the hot wooden jetty, waiting for the restaurant boat to take her back to the yacht. She knew she should call Marcus, but the thought of talking about what she had just seen made her feel sick.

Through the slats in the wood she could see small shoals of fish darting amongst the shallows. Cate shaded her eyes and looked out across the blue sea, her mind churning as she tried to make sense of what had just happened. *Catwalk II* was still there, a thing of glistening beauty as it pivoted on its moorings but it no longer felt like a safe berth against the world.

While she made the journey, Cate hoped to be able to slip back onboard unnoticed and go straight to find Marcus. It would be easier to tell him her story face to face. But, as the restaurant boat approached the side of the yacht, she could see activity on the top deck. A few metres out, the pilot cut the engine on the little boat and drifted gently and expertly up to the steps on the rear of *Catwalk II* where, to her horror, Bill was waiting to grab the rope.

'Hi, Cate,' said Bill cheerfully. 'Good afternoon?'

It took all Cate's inner strength to push down the knot of nausea in her stomach. It wouldn't do to throw up on Bill's shiny deck shoes, she thought wryly, although it was the least he deserved. But any flicker of emotion, any clue or hint that she had changed in her attitude towards Bill could, she knew, prove disastrous – if not fatal.

'I got distracted shopping,' she said, trying to sound enthusiastic. 'You know what us girls are like. Bought this dress. Do you like it?'

She looked at Bill's smiling face, and Cate had a vision of the Professor pleading for his life, trying to talk to Bill, to reason with him or offer him a bargain that would keep him alive. Or perhaps Bill had shot him without warning, coming up behind him and taking him by surprise.

'Marcus was asking for you,' said Bill as Cate scrambled up onto the hot white deck. 'He wants some help in the kitchen.'

'On my way,' said Cate gratefully. *Clever old Marcus*, she

thought. He would know she needed an excuse to talk to him.

'Not so fast, buddy,' said Bill, turning to face her full on. Her heart flipped – had Bill somehow found out about her adventures earlier in the day? 'I need you up in the pilot's bay first,' he said briskly. 'I've got a problem ordering some parts and I need you to talk to the guy at the chandlery shop. It's pretty cool having my own personal translator around. You know how rubbish I am at any foreign language.'

Oh yeah? thought Cate, forcing herself to smile back at him. *Like your fluent Russian?*

Half an hour later, Cate left the pilot's bay, almost reeling with the effort of having to spend time in a confined space with Bill. His every move made her jumpy, she read double meanings into his words and felt sick when he came up close to her. But if Bill noticed any change in her behaviour he didn't show any sign of it. Cate carried out her job – ordering some obscure fuel pump parts from a grumpy Frenchman – with success.

All the while Bill was so funny and friendly, cheerful and kind that, more than once, Cate caught herself wondering if she had somehow imagined the events of the day, or even if Bill had a double. But perhaps that was the sign of a real psychopath, someone who could switch from kind to killer without ever once betraying himself to the outside world.

As she finally headed towards the galley she could hear music and laughter coming from on the top deck. Nancy and Tass were clearly back and in party mode, entertaining the group of glamorous-looking people that they had met on the beach after lunch.

'OK,' said Marcus urgently, shutting the door of the galley behind her. 'I've been waiting for you to call me. Tell me what happened today.'

Cate was terrified that if she told him she would start to cry and never stop. Eventually, she remembered her phone. She pulled it out and motioned Marcus to come over, looking up at him mutely as she began to flip through the pictures.

As the macabre slideshow came to an end, he touched her gently on the shoulder. 'Who was it, Cate?' he asked, in such a quiet voice that she hardly heard him. 'Do you know who did this – who shot him?'

Cate turned to him with a look of utter misery. 'Bill,' she said flatly. 'Bill killed him.'

CHAPTER 11

Marcus stared back at her, stunned. 'Cate, are you sure?'

'You asked me to check out anyone who left the restaurant, so I did,' she said, her voice dull and low. 'Bill said he was going shopping, but he went to that house and went inside and I heard the shot. I broke in and I found, I found . . .'

Marcus waited patiently.

'I found the professor and he was only just dead. No one else went in or out of that house – it could only have been Bill who shot him. But just now he was talking, chatting, laughing like nothing had happened.' She gulped and Marcus gave her a hug.

'God, Cate, I'm so sorry,' he said. 'But please, I have to know everything,'

She told him, as simply as she could, and then turned to him again in terror. 'I nearly died, Marcus, right there in the house. I was nearly blown to pieces.' She was crying properly now, hot tears running down her cheeks. 'It's OK, Marcus,' she continued, half laughing at his startled expression. 'I don't make a habit of blubbing. It's just that it was pretty scary back there and I thought that if I died no one would have ever known how it happened or even find my body. It would have been so awful for my family.'

'Pretty rough for you, too.' Marcus smiled at her ruefully.

'But it's over now, yeah?' Cate asked eagerly. 'You can arrest Bill.'

Marcus shook his head. 'I wish it were that simple,' he said, 'but we still have too many questions unanswered. For a start, Bill could just be a hired hit man who knows nothing about the animals.

'To crack this, we have to map the complete chain from start to finish. Who is behind this animal smuggling, who's funding it and why, what are they really doing with those animals and where are they now. If we pull Bill in too soon he'll shut up like a clam, and we'll never know.' Marcus suddenly looked exhausted and careworn. He rubbed at the dark patches under his eyes and then turned to face her full on.

'Cate, you have done an awesome job,' he said. 'Beyond my wildest expectations. I hate to do this to you but I have to ask you to dig deep and to keep going for a little while longer.'

Cate looked at him in disbelief. 'Jeez, Marcus, didn't you hear me?' she said angrily. 'It was bad enough searching Nancy's room with Ahmed breathing down my neck. I've been in fights with assassins and nearly been blown up by a bomb. My luck isn't going to hold out much longer and if I learnt one thing today it's that actually I would quite like to live.'

Marcus sighed. 'We still need proof of who is involved and we need to find those animals. I'm sorry, Cate, with or without you the case is far from over. But with you we have a far, far better chance of solving it quickly and before any one else gets killed.'

The room fell quiet. Cate stared at Marcus as she tried to work out what to do next. She was just about to speak when there was a loud and anguished scream from upstairs.

She and Marcus raced for the door and took the stairs to the upper deck three at a time. As they reached the top deck, Cate saw Nancy surrounded by her new-found, and now clearly very embarrassed, friends who were gradually backing away from her.

She was gripping her mobile phone in a shaking hand. As she spotted Cate and Marcus she began to howl again. 'The scumbag termites!' She forced the words out between her sobs. 'The parasites!'

'She got a call from her agent,' one of the guests whispered fearfully. 'I think it's bad news.'

'Nancy,' Cate spoke calmly, reaching out to touch the distraught woman on the arm. 'Nancy, what's happened?'

Nancy turned slowly towards Cate, grabbing at her hand so tightly that Cate winced. 'It's the newspapers,' Nancy said in a whisper. 'They've got a pic of me dancing up close with Tass on that table and have run it next to a picture of my kids being taken to school yesterday by their nanny in the rain looking all miserable and sad. They're saying I'm an unfit mother. They've even got a quote from the bleeding Ramibian ambassador saying that my adoption papers for Beech should be withdrawn. The cheek of the man!' Her voice took on an indignant tone. 'He didn't say that when I coughed up for a playground for every village in his godforsaken dumpsville of a country.'

'It must be awful for you,' said Cate, 'but no one will really believe that.'

'Of course they will believe it.' Lulu had a glacial look on her face as she stepped out of the crowd. 'What about all those stores that have agreed to stock your organic children's cosmetics? Great timing, Nancy!'

Nancy stared at her PA incredulously before collapsing dramatically into the arms of the nearest man.

Lulu continued, 'That's why I'm just about to book flights for all five of your children. They break up from school next week anyway so a few days won't make any difference. They'll be with us first thing tomorrow morning, followed shortly by a photographer friend of mine who will be doing some quick paparazzi shots of your lovely, warm, family holiday. The pictures will be leaked to the papers tomorrow evening and will be on everyone's breakfast table the next morning. And tomorrow's plans will have to change.'

Nancy pushed the arms of her willing comforter away. 'Lulu,' she said, her face shining from her tears. 'Lulu, you're a diamond. Right guys, the party is back on.'

'This is going to be fun,' said Wendy sarcastically, sitting with a notebook in front of her in the downstairs mess. Around the table a crisis meeting was taking place which included Cate, Marcus, Lulu and Jules. Mikey was there to help out on security while, much to Cate's relief, Bill was back upstairs, preparing to take the boat back to Antibes.

'We've got about twelve hours to make this boat child-proof, to work out menus, sleeping arrangements and child care,' she continued.

'No nannies coming?' said Jules, looking horrified.

'No nannies,' confirmed Lulu, filing her nails. 'One is on holiday back in New York, the Bulgarian one had to rush home because someone was on their death bed and the one left on duty has just this minute texted me her notice. She's going to put the five of them on the plane and never wants to see any of us again. Thank God I got her to sign a confidentiality clause.'

'So that means, until we can get hold of another nanny, it's just us,' confirmed Wendy. 'Well, food should be easy enough. Marcus, stock up on the frozen chips and nuggets and chocolate mini rolls.'

'Not so fast,' snapped Lulu. 'Have you forgotten? Since she wrote that parenting book Nancy now insists that her children follow an organic, carefully balanced diet with a minimum of meat, no additives and definitely, definitely no sweets or sugar. Oak is allergic to eggs, by the way. Elm can't eat any dairy, Ash reacts badly to gluten and little Willow hates citrus fruits. Beech is only two – will she need a bottle?'

'In South Africa plenty of the kids would be happy to eat what they were given,' said Wendy dryly. 'Marcus can you cope with all those dietary whatsits?'

'Sure,' said Marcus, valiantly trying not to laugh. 'Chicken and chips for breakfast it is.'

'Good – I think,' said Wendy doubtfully. 'Now, Jules can move into the crew quarters and the five kids can share two cabins on the main deck.' There was a gasp of horror from Jules which everyone ignored.

'Now, childcare,' Wendy continued. 'I've arranged for a stand-in nanny from a local agency but she won't be with us for a day or so. Now I'm going to be busy housekeeping. Which leaves . . .'

There was a silence as everyone turned to look at Cate.

'Me?' she said incredulously. 'Not me. I've never babysat in my life. I don't even think I like kids. Especially not toddlers. And I wouldn't know one end of a nappy from another if it hit me on the head.'

'It might well do just that,' Marcus teased.

'Look, Cate,' said Wendy, putting on her reasonable tone. 'You're nearer in age to them than any of us. You must remember what it was like to be a child and, in any case, it's better than making beds and cleaning. Enjoy! Have fun on the beach, take them out for the day, buy them ice lollies – that kind of thing. We'll all help out when we can and we'll give you a really good allowance.'

Mikey shifted in his seat. 'Tass said to tell you that the kids can come onto his yacht for a day so that he and Nancy can get some peace,' he said flatly. 'Ride on the power boat, go on the golf range, have the run of the cinema and the gaming room, that kind of thing. Any use?'

Wendy looked at Cate. Marcus was looking at her too, and now his expression was deadly serious. She knew exactly what he was thinking – *The Good Times*. This was far too good an opportunity to miss.

She feigned reluctance but inside her heart was racing. 'Oh,

OK,' she said, still trying to sound as if her arm was being twisted.

'Good girl.' Wendy leant over and gave her arm a squeeze. 'Now, guys, let's get to it. Cate, the kids are due in at eight tomorrow morning so I suggest you get an early night and we'll see to the aftermath of the party.'

Three hours later, *Catwalk II* was nosing quietly through the inky black sea back towards the bay of Cannes. Finally, up ahead of them, the battlements of Antibes loomed out of the darkness.

The engines slowed as Bill began the tricky job of negotiating his way around the super yachts that were too vast to be moored in the marina and Cate amused herself by looking at the names and guessing who was rich enough to own them. Then suddenly, she realised, with a start, she was looking up at the blood red colours of *The Good Times*. The boat was easily one hundred metres long, dwarfing *Catwalk II* with its five-storey height, and Cate counted twenty-five portholes on the lowest deck alone.

Perched on the top deck, a black helicopter stood silent, and ten metres below it, a hoist held a sleek powerboat ready to be lowered into the sea at a moment's notice.

'I'll see you later,' Cate said quietly to the boat as *Catwalk II* slid slowly by.

Cate locked the door to her cabin and turned on her laptop. Her room was stuffy and hot, but she didn't dare open the portholes in case someone was within hearing. It was late, but with any luck Arthur would still have his computer on.

'Hi, Cate, great to see you. I was beginning to worry.'

Arthur was in his pyjamas but still wearing his glasses. 'God, you look shattered.'

'Thanks,' said Cate ruefully. 'That's because I nearly got blown up today. Arthur, get recording while I tell you about my day at the office.'

'Jeez!' said her brother as she finally got to the end of the day's events. His face had gone pale. 'Cate! What next?'

'Very good question,' said Cate. 'I'm not really sure. I was about to give up on being an agent. It's a lot more stressful than you'd think.'

The two of them grinned at each other.

'But then Nancy's kids are turning up tomorrow and because of them I'm getting a day on *The Good Times* and now I think I have to carry on. It's like someone up there is dangling this opportunity at me and I feel that, if I turned my back on it, well, I would always regret that I didn't see it through.'

'Cate,' said Arthur, putting on his persuasive tone of voice. 'Cate, you are sixteen years old. You should be, I don't know, going to the cinema, snogging boys, having rows with Dad and Monique about staying out late. You definitely should not be taking on murderers or playing at being a female James Bond. Leave that to the professionals. It's their job not yours.'

Cate smiled at him reassuringly. 'Don't worry, bro. I've managed to stay alive so far. And . . . it's kind of addictive.'

'Right,' said Arthur glumly.

'Remember, no telling Dad unless I don't call or text twice a day. Have you managed to find out anything more about Ramibia?'

It was Arthur's turn to look sheepish. 'Well, actually I did spend a bit of time poking around the Ramibian National Government system. I don't know who they got to fix their online security, but it leaks like a sieve. The password was only twenty-seven digits long. It took me all of forty minutes to crack.' He sounded disappointed.

'Move on, Arthur,' said Cate cheerfully.

'Yes, sorry, where was I? Well, working on the theory that most crimes are committed because of money, I went straight to accounts. I found out that in each of the separate ministries – finance, housing, transport and so on – there was a separate little account fund accessed only by the minister concerned. Actually, in most cases, they weren't so very little. The trade minister in charge of natural minerals is sitting on a slush fund in excess of thirty million dollars. Not bad for a bloke who was running a chain of fake sportswear shops just a few years ago.'

'And . . .' Cate prompted.

'Yeah, sorry. Well, the ministry of science and medicine is the one we're interested in. If there was something dodgy going on with animals they'd be in on it. And guess what I found?'

'Go on,' said Cate eagerly.

Arthur was enjoying himself. 'In the last year alone, ten separate payments had come into the minister's slush fund from a British registered charity called Survival Worldwide. Payments totalling over one and a half million euros. A quick Google job, and hey presto! Guess who is the founder, figurehead and the main benefactor of Survival Worldwide? Your boss, Nancy.'

Arthur paused, savouring the look of shock on his sister's face. 'That's not all. Really big money came in from a bank in

Russia too. Tens of millions of euros. I can't trace the actual account, but I did manage to discover that the bank was owned by Mr Taplinski Senior. In other words, Tass's dad.'

Cate's mind was racing. 'Let me get this straight,' she said slowly. 'Nancy, and probably Tass, are putting large sums of money into a fund for the minister in charge of science and medicine – presumably animal medicine as well – in one of the most lawless countries in the world. That's great work, Arthur, but I haven't a clue why they are doing it.'

'Me neither,' said Arthur cheerfully. 'There's more. With all the other ministry accounts, the money tends to come in from whoever is paying the kickback and then goes out again to just one person, the minister. It's straight into his back pocket. But this account is different. Sure, the minister is taking a fifty per cent cut, but the rest of the money is going to another account based at the Bank of Tendo. We need to find out who holds that account.'

'So what's the problem?' asked Cate. 'Why can't you tell me now?'

'It's carefully protected by several passwords and complex security systems,' said Arthur admiringly. 'I'll keep trying.'

'OK,' Cate said doubtfully. 'But please be careful. Now I really need to get some kip.'

At eight o'clock sharp the next morning, Cate was standing at the bottom of the gangplank watching as a gaggle of children shepherded by a very harassed-looking taxi driver made their way towards her. The smallest child, a cherubic infant with curly hair and huge brown eyes, was being carried by the middle-aged man and as he reached Cate he almost dropped the child into her arms.

'*Un, deux, trois, quatre, cinq,*' he rattled off. Large sweat patches were visible under his armpit. 'All yours, *mademoiselle. Bon chance.*' And then he was gone, leaving Cate in charge.

'Hello,' said Cate, as the five children eyed her up and down. 'My name's Cate. I'll be looking after you for the next few days.'

The children stared back at her, silent. Then all hell let loose.

'Cuddles needs a wee,' shouted a small boy who was carrying a rucksack and a teddy bear.

'I feel sick,' said a blond-haired girl.

'Where's Mum?' demanded the oldest child.

The little girl in Cate's arms began to smell rather unpleasant.

'Let's take our shoes off and go aboard,' said Cate weakly, grabbing at another child who was skipping perilously close to the side. 'Fancy some breakfast?'

CHAPTER 12

It took Cate half an hour to restore calm. Nancy was still fast asleep and, as she hadn't left instructions to be woken up when the children arrived, no one quite had the nerve to do so. Instead, with the help of Wendy, Cate had changed her first nappy relatively successfully, Marcus had taken the boys to the loo and now all five children were sitting around the large table in the salon munching their way noisily through cereal and bacon sandwiches.

'What about the carefully balanced diet?' Cate whispered to Marcus who screwed up his face and put his finger to his lips in reply.

Now they were quiet, Cate could take stock and try to work out who was who. The oldest child, Oak, was an Asian boy of about ten. He sat quietly but Cate caught him observing everything that was going on around him. *A sharp cookie*, she thought.

Elm, an African boy and his sister, Ash, were, Cate realised, the seven-year-old twins from the Congo. Five-year-old Willow looked Eastern European with her green eyes and round, high cheek-boned face and the toddler, Beech was, Cate knew, an orphan from Ramibia.

'Oak,' said Cate, hesitantly. 'Do you think your brother and sisters would like to go to the beach?'

Before he could answer, Nancy was in the salon, in full maternal mode.

'Darlings!' she cried as the children looked up in amazement. 'Darlings! Come to Mummy.' She crouched down and held out her arms. Elm and Ash rushed to her and were rewarded with a huge hug, a very tired Willow made it in third place and Cate carried a sleeping Beech over to her mother who stroked the child's hair.

'Aren't you coming for a hug, Oak, babe?' Nancy said, looking relieved as Oak eventually presented the top of his head for a kiss.

Chattering away to her brood she bustled off towards the outside deck, Cate trailing behind them, still carrying Beech. She was surprised by how natural Nancy was with her children and she felt bad that she had assumed otherwise.

'Aren't they gorgeous?' Nancy said to Cate as she cuddled Beech. 'I sometimes forget how lucky I am.'

'They're great,' agreed Cate. 'I think I'm going to enjoy looking after them.'

They smiled at each other.

'I wish Tass felt the same way,' Nancy suddenly blurted out. 'He ignores them or shouts at them. It makes me so sad. I can't see how we can have a future when he doesn't want to be with my kids.'

Cate was silent. She knew there was more to come.

'It's the way he's been brought up you see. I came from a back-to-back in Catford where all us kids saw our mum and dad all the time. Sick of the sight of each other sometimes. But Tass, he grew up with nannies and saw his parents once a week if he was lucky. Our holidays in Clacton were the best part of the year in our house, apart from Christmas. Tass can't even remember one holiday with his parents. His nanny took him instead. Can you imagine?'

Cate shook her head.

'He doesn't even have any proper brothers and sisters. They're all half-brother this, and stepsister that and they wouldn't even recognise each other if they passed in the street. Not one of his family ever came to watch him play tennis. It was always his coach or his fitness trainer or his agents, all of them paid for by Tass, of course.'

'Is that where you met him?' Cate asked. 'Watching tennis?'

Nancy laughed. 'No way, babe, I hate sport. I only go to the big tournaments like Wimbledon for the publicity, and Tass never got that far.' She smiled fondly. 'We met at a party in a castle somewhere in Italy. It was a friend of Lulu who invited us. She knows loads of people.

'Tass was standing there surrounded by all these trashy girls and I was with Lulu and Jules and some other guys. Lulu must have seen us eyeing each other up, 'cos she took the bull by the horns, went over to Tass and the next thing he and me were dancing and chatting and that was that.'

'Love at first sight,' said Cate solemnly.

'Yeah, that's right.' Nancy looked wistful. Then her eyes filled with tears. She spoke quietly, though the children were busy exploring the deck and paying no attention to their mother. 'We've had such a great time but recently it's all been going wrong. He's in a bad mood all the time now. It's his old man's fault. He's ignored him for most of his life, but suddenly he's on the blower telling Tass what a failure he is, that it's time he got a decent career and showed he was his father's son.

'I try to be supportive. I say, "Tass, tell him where to get off", but he never does. It's not just all about the money. He still wants to please him, doesn't he? He still wants to make daddy proud.' She fell silent.

'Parents, huh?' said Cate, trying to cheer her up. 'I haven't spoken to my mum in weeks and I know that when she does ring up she'll want something. Usually it's to get me to ask Dad for some more money for her so she can go on another mad self-enlightenment course!'

Nancy smiled then. 'I like you, Cate,' she said. 'You're what my nan would call a sensible girl. I'm glad you're looking after my kids.'

'Me too,' said Cate. She meant it.

'And don't worry about Tass,' Nancy continued. 'He may be a bit stressy but he's a diamond underneath.'

Cate must have looked doubtful. 'No, Cate, he is,' Nancy insisted. 'He's really kind to me. He might not be good with kids but he helps with my charities. Big time. He introduced me to this really clever bloke – he's like a famous professor, although I'd never heard of him, but now we're kind of working together.'

Her voice dropped to a whisper and she began to rock Beech on her lap. 'I can't tell you what it is but me and Tass, we're working on something right now that will change the world forever.' She looked at Cate's expression and misread it for one of disbelief. 'No really. It'll sort of save the planet. Well, some of it. Then his dad can go take a running jump.'

Cate was desperate to ask more questions, but just as she was thinking how to do it without arousing Nancy's suspicions, Beech started to whimper which quickly turned into an ear-splitting howl.

'Well,' said Cate, reluctantly giving up on the idea, 'the kids have been up since five so the little ones could probably do with a nap. Perhaps Oak and the twins should just chill out and watch TV for a bit.'

She took the two youngest children to their cabin, put them into their pyjamas, washed faces and hands and then tucked them up into the clean, crisp sheets. Within minutes of dimming the lights they were asleep. Oak and the twins were happily settled in front of the big TV in the larger of the guest bedrooms.

Back up on the main deck, a clatter of footsteps and loud voices heralded the arrival of Tass, Mikey and Ahmed, the former clearly in a very grumpy mood.

'Here comes the Earth Mother,' he mocked as Nancy gave him a kiss. 'Have you adopted another baby this morning or are we slipping?'

'All right, Tass, darling.' Nancy was placatory. 'They're all nice and quiet. You and I can go and have a nap as well if you like.'

'Great idea,' said Tass, cheering up. 'It was a late one last night. But, Nancy, no kids this evening, OK? I want you all to myself.'

Nancy hesitated, looking at Cate in a 'What did I tell you?' kind of way.

'Perhaps Nancy could have tea with them and then I'll take them to the beach this evening while you have dinner?' Cate offered.

'Fab idea, Cate,' said Nancy, looking at Tass for approval.

'Tea? Monkey's tea party more likely,' he grumbled in his strange drawl. 'Yeah. That sounds reasonable. What about tomorrow?'

It was Cate's moment and she seized it. 'Er, Mikey mentioned that perhaps I could take them onto *The Good Times*,' she said timidly. 'You know, they could have a go on the powerboat, perhaps swim in the pool?'

'Did he?' Tass turned to Cate, his face black. 'I think he meant to say that the kids were welcome. I don't let anyone onboard my boat without full security clearance.'

'Awww, Tass,' said Nancy plaintively. 'Come on, that's not true. You didn't check up on me, babe.'

'Oh yes I did,' said Tass calmly.

Nancy looked shocked but gamely carried on. 'If you want the kids on the boat then Cate has to go with them,' she said firmly. 'Who else will look after them? Would Ahmed change Beech's nappies? Cate's only a kid. Stop being so paranoid, darling.'

Suddenly a loud wailing came from the direction of the cabins and a small tousled figure came trailing out onto the deck.

'Nappy poo poo,' said Beech, heading for the nearest adult who just happened to be Tass. 'Smelly poo,' she said with satisfaction as she hugged Tass's bare knees.

He prised her off disdainfully and pushed her towards Cate. 'No way are these kids going to be hanging around here tomorrow,' he said. 'They can go on *The Good Times* and as far as I am concerned they can stay on *The Good Times*. But just make sure you clean up after them, OK, Cate? And leave your mobile here – I don't want you taking photos or anything.'

Cate waited for Tass and Nancy to go before picking up Beech and giving her a cuddle. She didn't even care about the dreadful smell coming from her nappy. 'Clever girl,' she whispered quietly into her dainty little ear.

That evening, sitting on the narrow crescent of sand which ran alongside the city walls, Cate watched as the children splashed and played happily in the still warm waters.

The twins were building a sandcastle and, just a few metres away from Cate, the younger two were amusing themselves by running away from the waves. Oak had been swimming in the shallows then he came and lay down in the evening sunshine next to Cate.

'Looking forward to going on *The Good Times* tomorrow?' Cate asked him.

'I guess so,' said Oak, his face buried in the towel. 'Been on it before you know. At Christmas.'

'Lucky you,' said Cate. 'It has everything, doesn't it – a cinema, a big pool . . . even a submarine?'

'Yes,' replied Oak. 'But we didn't get to see the submarine.'

'Hmm, that's a shame. Oak, do you have a mobile phone?' asked Cate casually.

'Yes, of course,' he said. 'I'm sure I brought it to Antibes.'

'Would you do me a huge, huge favour?' asked Cate. 'Tass is clearly pretty hot on security and I'm not allowed to take my phone on his boat tomorrow, but I've got to make a call, a really urgent call.'

'To a boy?' asked Oak, turning his face towards her. 'You've got a boyfriend, then?'

'Not exactly,' said Cate, smiling at him. 'But could you take your phone onboard for me to use anyway?'

'No probs,' Oak said. 'I'll take it. Don't worry, your secret's safe with me. Who's that guy?'

Cate followed Oak's line of vision and saw with a shock Michel coming towards them. The other evening he had been dressed in jeans and T-shirt, tonight he was wearing black tie, his bow still hanging untied around his neck, his white dress shirt open at the top.

'We have to stop meeting like this,' he said, sitting down on the towel next to Cate.

'You look very smart,' said Cate, not knowing what else to say.

'A-ha,' said Michel. 'Thank you. Tonight I am playing at the wedding anniversary of the mayor of Antibes. It is a very smart party. What a shame I can't take a guest.'

He smiled at Cate and she felt her stomach lurch.

'How did you know I was here?' she said weakly.

'I asked at your boat of course,' he said, seemingly surprised she wouldn't know.

There was a silence. The setting sun lit up the hairs on

Michel's forearms, turning them a golden brown.

'Cate,' said Michel slowly. 'I know you are very busy but I wondered . . .'

'Yes?' said Cate, trying to be brave enough to look him in the eye and failing.

'How about we organise this drink?'

'You can ask her out but she's already talking to some bloke tomorrow on the phone.'

Cate had forgotten Oak was still lying on the towel next to them. Her face burnt with embarrassment. 'He's just a friend.'

Michel didn't seem fazed. 'I am not surprised Cate has men calling her. She is very pretty.' He grinned at Oak who got up and wandered back down to the water just as Beech and Willow came rushing back up to sit on Cate's lap. 'I can see I will have to stop messing around.' He turned to Cate, his face serious again. 'Cate, can I have you to myself one evening very soon. Perhaps for dinner? Sunday?'

Cate nodded happily. The boys she knew were never like this. If they fancied you they usually got their mates to ask you out and then it was fifty-fifty whether or not they were doing it for a joke. And if it did get as far as a date, well, it was a walk in the park and a quick snog at the end of it.

'Great,' said Cate. 'Thanks. I could do with some time away from everyone on the boat. They're great but, well, they are all a bit older than me.'

Michel laughed. 'Don't worry. I promise to take you somewhere where no one over twenty-five is allowed! And now I must go, or I will be late for my date with the Mayor.'

He stood up and Cate stood up with him. He gave her a

quick, gentle kiss on the cheek and was gone, striding barefoot over the sand, his polished black shoes in one hand, his other raised in a gesture of farewell.

Cate sat back down again, waving her hand in front of her face to cool herself down. *Wow*, she thought to herself. *If only my friends could see me now!*

CHAPTER 13

Cate woke up early, with an excited churning in the pit of her stomach. She lay still in her bunk, trying to work out why, and then she remembered. Today she was headed to the epicentre of this case, to *The Good Times*.

Cate lay in bed working out what to take with her. Although she would have access to Oak's phone, that would be no good to her without her own contacts. Suddenly she had a brainwave. All she needed was the information contained on her sim card. As long as she took that with her, any old phone – including Oak's – would do the job.

Then there was Marcus's survival pack. She would be mad to leave it behind but, although the tin was small, it wasn't invisible. She could do something about that too. She hunted through her belongings and brought out a small, unopened box of Tampax. She slid open the lid and pulled out the tubes and, when it was empty, pushed the survival tin, together with her sim card, into the bottom of the cardboard box. It was a perfect fit. Next she used her penknife to cut the tampons in half and placed them back in the packet on top of the tin. If any man was brave enough to check the box, they would find a full packet of tampons. She grinned to herself. There were definitely some advantages to being a woman.

Finally she considered the gun, still hidden in the freezer, and made a mental note to find another hiding place for it soon. In the meantime, Cate was sorely tempted by the idea of creeping across the corridor to retrieve it to take with her. But if the guards did find it on her – as they probably would – she would be in so much trouble it didn't bear thinking about.

By seven-thirty her backpack was ready. As well as the survival kit, she had thrown in a jumble of girly stuff – mascara, flip flops, hairbrush and a spare T-shirt – in a bid to distract any prying eyes. Then she had showered, dried her hair and was now starving.

The silence as she made her way through the middle deck meant that the children and Nancy were still fast asleep and Cate headed for the kitchen.

Ten minutes later she was up on the top deck with Marcus, sitting in the sunshine, eating her way through several freshly warmed croissants plastered with a gorgeous blueberry jam and drinking a large mug of English tea.

'I hear you have a boyfriend,' he teased, swinging his long legs over a lounger and pulling it up close to Cate.

She blushed. 'How on earth do you know about Michel?'

'Well, you see,' said Marcus seriously, 'anyone who comes

into contact with you has to be vetted at the highest level.'

Cate stared at him in horror.

'We have had tabs on your Michel since you bumped into him at the nightclub.'

He let her suffer for a minute before breaking into his now familiar giggles. 'Sorry, Cate, couldn't resist it. Of course we're not following him. Try explaining that particular expense to Henri. No, he came to the boat yesterday asking for you and Wendy told me about him. He's very good-looking,' he added.

'Mmm,' said Cate, trying hard not to laugh too.

Suddenly Marcus was serious. He went to the top of the spiral staircase, checking that no one was coming up. Then he took Cate by the hand, walked her over to the jacuzzi and switched it on. The pump whirred loudly into action, the froth rising quickly out of the large tub.

'We can talk now,' said Marcus.

'According to Arthur, Nancy's charity and Tass's father's bank are donating a small fortune to the Ramibian Ministry of science and medicine,' said Cate slowly. 'All back-pocket stuff, of course. We know some of it is a bribe, but part of it is going into another account. Arthur is trying to work out who owns it.'

'Wow,' said Marcus admiringly.

'And Nancy let slip yesterday that Tass was helping her with some amazing save-the-planet scheme. Something that would make him into a bit of a hero. It's to impress his dad apparently. And guess what?' Cate went on. 'She and the professor definitely knew each other. More than knew each other. They were working together, probably with Tass,

165

although I couldn't find out anything more about it.

'From the way she was talking about him in the present tense, she doesn't know he's dead either. Unless, of course, she was putting on a very good act.'

Marcus nodded thoughtfully. Then it was his turn. 'Cate, yesterday, when you were on the beach I searched through Bill's stuff. I checked everywhere, even the engine room, but I couldn't find anything incriminating. We've had a tail on him though. Last night he told me he was going out to meet some yachtie mates. Well, they might have been mates but they weren't yachties.

'He took an inflatable dinghy out to *The Good Times*. As you know, that damn yacht has more security on it than Air Force One. If they hadn't recognised the dinghy he was in, particularly at night, they would have sent out an armed response unit to investigate.'

'But they didn't?' asked Cate.

'No,' said Marcus. 'They knew he was coming all right. They didn't even search him when he climbed aboard, let alone check over the laptop he took out of his rucksack.'

'Laptop?' Cate's mind raced back to the sound of the moped being revved, Bill coming out of the doomed house carrying the bright blue laptop under his arm.

'Yes, it was the blue laptop. Your job is to find out just why Bill was prepared to kill to get it.'

At ten o'clock sharp, a dark red, open-decked powerboat, with Mikey and Ahmed on board, nosed its way alongside the *Catwalk II*.

Nancy appeared in a short silk dressing gown to wave the children off. She looked glum, tired and older than her thirty years and Cate, remembering their conversation of the previous day, suddenly felt desperately sorry for her.

'Don't worry, we'll have a great time,' she said gently to Nancy. 'And I'm sure you'll have a fab day as well.'

Now all the children were fitted with life jackets and safely aboard and Ahmed gestured impatiently for Cate to clamber onto the powerboat too. As she did so, Beech shook herself free from Ahmed, toddled over and snuggled onto her now familiar position on Cate's lap. Willow planted a sticky kiss on her lips, and Cate looked back to see Nancy's stricken face as she waved her children goodbye. Could this woman really be involved in an international ring smuggling beautiful animals?

The wind was low and the sea calm. It was a perfect ten-minute ride out from the harbour. Suddenly *The Good Times* was looming above them, its tall sides blocking out the sunshine and, despite the heat and the bright blue sea, Cate felt her mood sinking.

She'd texted Arthur that morning, but she felt sick as she thought about the task ahead. A lot could happen in the twelve hours before she was due to text again. Suddenly she wished that she was anywhere else, even back at home in London in the rain, gossiping to Louisa about what their mates were up to.

Then she pulled herself together.

Treat it like an exam, she told herself. *It's worst beforehand, not so bad during and great when it's all over.*

Now the pilot was cutting his engines and the low wall at

the rear of the super yacht slowly opened to allow the powerboat to drift quietly over a small watery ramp into a mini harbour. It came to a gentle halt next to three jetskis and a ski boat. Cate shook her head in amazement.

'All aboard,' said Mikey from the small platform. Cate took a deep breath, resisted the urge to ask for a lift straight back to the *Catwalk II*, and lifted Beech carefully onto the walkway. With Ahmed still on board, the powerboat reversed and headed back out. Clearly Tass wasn't allowed to be without protection for even a few hours.

With Mikey in the lead, the small party walked silently into a tunnel which led towards a lift.

'The stairs are over in that corner,' grunted Mikey to Cate. 'The lift isn't really for staff, but as you're with the kids you can use it for now.'

The heavily carpeted lift whirred silently upwards for what seemed like far too long and, as the doors opened, Cate realised that they were on the top deck, twenty metres above the sea. The view out to the horizon was breathtaking.

Directly in front of her was the helicopter landing pad and beyond that was what looked like a glass dance floor, studded with lights and edged by a horseshoe shaped bar and huge sound system. Beyond that stood the bridge, surrounded by heavily tinted windows edged with black blinds, no doubt waiting to drop in an instant.

Through the open door Cate clocked an array of controls and screens that wouldn't have looked out of place in a NASA launch pad. From its roof, a radar mast reached up into the sky, its horizontal listening arm rotating through never-ending circles. And next to it . . . no, it couldn't be.

'Watch out for the missiles.' Mikey followed her gaze. 'Up there, above the bridge.'

'Bit over the top, isn't it?' Cate tried to sound casual. 'All this security. What are they expecting? World War III?'

Mikey sighed, clearly exasperated by her naivity. 'You've got no idea, girl,' he said. 'It's all lovely here, I grant you, but out there in the big, bad world there are all sorts of people who would just love to get their hands on this yacht – and the people who own it.

'Mr Taplinski does a lot of business in Africa and sometimes we sail there. Even you must have heard about the pirates that are taking vessels and holding them for millions of dollars of ransom. The only thing that will scare them off is a missile over their bows.'

Cate nodded. She had heard of the pirates. But she wondered too, whether there wasn't another more sinister motive behind the fear. Maybe all this armoury wasn't about stopping people coming on the boat as much as keeping something trapped here instead.

By now Oak and the twins were running screaming with delight towards the large figure-of-eight swimming pool at the prow of the deck. A palm tree clad island and a bridge stood at the crossover point and at the far end were several water slides and a fountain to swim under. Inflatable dinghies, a blow up crocodile and some boogie boards bobbed on the surface.

'There's a wave machine and a sound system too,' explained Mikey.

'Any chance of a guided tour later?' said Cate innocently, holding hands tightly with Willow and Beech to make sure they didn't follow their siblings to the pool without her. 'Not often a girl like me gets chances to look around a boat like this.'

Mikey looked at her, considering her request. 'Not being nosy, are we?' he said. 'You haven't got a camera in that bag?'

'No,' said Cate, doing her best to sound outraged. 'You know Ahmed searched it earlier. It's OK, I was only asking. Oak wanted to see the submarine, but if it's all top secret then don't worry. I'll explain. Come on, kids, let's get changed.'

'Yeah, well,' Mikey said. 'It's a bleeding big yacht and we don't want you getting lost. I'll see what I can do.'

For the next hour the children were totally happy playing in the water. A lifeguard appeared and spent most of the time splashing around with a delighted Beech and Willow on his back, leaving Cate free to relax by the side of the pool.

It was paradise, thought Cate, as she sucked at an ice-cold Diet Coke with a straw. Except that, somewhere on this yacht, evil had been planned and carried out, perhaps was being carried out still. As Mikey had said, *The Good Times* was a bleeding big yacht. It could hide an awful lot of secrets. Including a laptop that contained details so precious that they may have cost a man his life. Despite the sunshine, Cate felt herself shiver.

Two minutes later, Mikey came hurrying up the stairs, followed by the boat pilot and three other men, all immaculate in stewards' uniforms.

Mikey beckoned Cate over towards him. 'Cate, we have to

go back,' he said quietly. 'There's some sort of security emergency going on, something to do with paparazzi trying to climb onto *Catwalk II*. Not sure it's too serious, but Tass wants to show them who's boss anyway. He's asked me to bring the security team back to them.'

Cate's heart sank. It looked like her golden opportunity was turning to dust. 'But we've only just got here,' she said, gesturing towards the children who were still playing.

'You can stay. José here and his crew can look after you.'

Cate tried to hide her delight but Mikey was desperate to get going, too hyped up for action to even notice her expression. 'We'll be back in a few hours. Be good.'

Oh, I'll be good all right, thought Cate to herself as she watched the powerboat bouncing low over the waves to Antibes harbour. Cate counted ten men on board including Mikey, all with a military look about them.

It's a small army, Cate realised with a start. *This boat isn't a superyacht. It's a floating fortress.*

But for now the fortress was without its private army.

'Can we have our tour of the boat now?' she asked José, gesturing to the children. 'They are very excited about it.'

'A tour? I didn't know about that.'

'Mikey did promise us,' said Cate, fluttering her eyelashes.

'Yes, he did.' Oak was at Cate's side, looking up pleadingly at José. 'He said we could see the submarine. I want to see the submarine. So does Elm and Ash and Willow. We've been looking forward to it for days.'

'Kids, huh?' José looked benignly at Cate. 'Let me decide about that, but first we can look around the boat.'

'Why not?' said Cate, picking up her rucksack. 'They could do with a break from the sun.'

Cate's head was soon reeling. They had walked through a vast salon with a sofa large enough to seat eight people and a dining table laid with gold-leafed crockery and cutlery for sixteen. The children had run around like lunatics in the ballroom and marvelled at the fish tanks set into the walls. Then, to squeals of delight, José had shown them the switches that slowly ratcheted back the dance floor to reveal another swimming pool, this one heated and complete with a jacuzzi.

The middle deck held the guest cabins, twelve in all, each with ensuite and a balcony so that they could enjoy the sea view as they travelled. Every room had its own theme – one was a beach hut on a tropical island, another the interior of a stately home complete with a velvet curtained four-poster bed. Perched above them all was the penthouse suite – a loft-style apartment which ran almost the entire length of the deck opening.

'The bed turns,' explained José, calling them into the room, 'so you can change the view or enjoy the sunshine. And here,' he gestured to Cate, 'is room for one hundred outfits and fifty pairs of shoes.'

Cate shook her head. 'Awesome,' she said finally. 'Truly, truly awesome.'

José shepherded them into the lift and down to the cinema complex. Oak tugged on his sleeve. 'José,' he said. 'I really, really want to see the submarine.'

'Submarine, submarine, submarine,' the others chanted.

'OK, OK,' José said. 'We'll go there now. But you must do as you are told, OK? There are lots of things that cannot be touched and rooms we must not go into. You promise?'

They nodded solemnly.

As the lift doors opened on the bottom level, it was as if they had entered another world. They were now in the bowels of a working ship where there was clearly no interest in luxuries. The floors were bare metal or lino, and the walls and ceilings painted a bright white, made even starker by the fluorescent lights which ran the length of the ceiling. Behind the lift, through some double doors, men were moving about in what was clearly the engine room, and huge, gleaming metal pipes ran from the engines along the length of the floor and up through the ceiling above. They were hot and steam came hissing through from joints in the piping. Cate felt as if she was in a factory.

'Stay away from the pipes,' she told the children, showing them the steam, and, surprisingly subdued, they obeyed.

Despite the piping and the fact that it was a hot summer's day, it was clammy and cold. 'We are now five metres under the sea,' said José, by way of explanation as he saw Cate rubbing her arms in a bid to warm up.

'Spooky,' said Willow, and Cate nodded.

'It is a bit,' she said, 'but José will look after us.'

The group made their way along the deck, Cate falling gradually behind as she did her best to absorb every tiny detail. Halfway down she spotted a bank of CCTV screens watched over by a middle-aged man wearing a pair of headphones, next to him a small wall-mounted screen beeped as red dots moved slowly to and fro. Cate looked questioningly at José.

'He is monitoring inside the boat and around the boat. The sonar system is here.'

Cate tried to look bored as she watched the screens out of the corner of her eye. On one screen she saw the swimming pool and inwardly shuddered at the knowledge that, whilst they had been splashing around, they had been watched by unseen eyes.

Strangely, Cate couldn't see the submarine bay on his screens. Did that mean it had its own security system, separate from the rest of the boat? If so, why?

Finally they came to a walled-off area with a pair of thick steel double doors. 'Through here is the submarine area,' said José, stopping by the doors. 'You all stay close to me or we will have to leave.'

Everyone nodded, Cate watching closely as José punched in a code.

Easy, thought Cate triumphantly, using her memory system once again. As they walked through the double doors she saw another door to her left. She made to go through it but José stopped her.

'No, no,' he said, shaking his head. 'You mustn't go into that room. And in any case,' he gestured at the security panel which was mounted on it, 'this can only be opened with a hand scan, after being authorised from that computer over there.'

He pointed down the corridor and Cate's heart sank. Virtually opposite the forbidden room a guard was sitting at a desk, staring at a computer screen. He looked up at them, barely concealing his irritation at their intrusion.

'He controls the doors,' explained José, 'to that room and to the submarine bay, but to get in you need special clearance.' The children looked at him wide-eyed and enthralled.

'Wow!' said Elm.

Cate turned to José, opening her eyes wide. 'So what's in that room?' she asked innocently. 'Is it something to do with the submarine? Or has he got the crown jewels in there?' She put on a girly giggle.

José shrugged. 'I don't know, miss. Not even I can get through.'

'But what happens when the guard goes to bed?' Oak asked. Cate was delighted. Exactly what she had wanted to know.

'Well, young man,' said José, 'then another man comes in. This room is never without a guard.'

Damn, thought Cate. *Damn, damn, damn.*

Her mind was reeling. She had to get into that room. It was the most secure and therefore clearly the most important room on the yacht, and it held who knew what secrets. Maybe even the key to the entire smuggling chain. She looked speculatively at the desk and the computer screen as they walked past. Two options were flashing up on the screen. *Room One. Room Two.*

As she watched, the guard clicked on *Room Two* and at the far end of the corridor a metal shutter, the size of a garage door, began to rise.

Thanks, mate, thought Cate to herself happily. Now she knew which room was which on the security system, and that was at least a start.

'This way, kids.' José was shooing them all towards the opening and now Cate could feel the temperature dropping further and could smell the salt water.

'The dockyard,' said José, dramatically gesturing into the darkness that lay beyond the metal doors. 'Don't get too close to the edge now.'

CHAPTER 14

'It's yellow!' The twins exclaimed as one. 'It's a yellow submarine.'

It lay partially submerged in the dark, gently lapping water, its shark-like nose facing away from them. The doorway was open and from it a wooden walkway had been laid over to the pontoon on which Cate and the children now stood.

It was indeed a bright, egg-yolk yellow, but the black-tinted portholes that lay just above the water level gave it a slightly sinister air. Beyond the submarine stood the bows of the yacht and into one side was cut a huge flap, pockmarked with riveted steel and dripping with water.

'The submarine entrance,' explained José to Oak. 'It is where the submarine enters and leaves the ship.'

'But why doesn't the boat sink when the hatch opens?' asked Oak.

'Good question,' said José kindly. 'When the submarine gets

ready to go out to sea, first of all the door we have just come through is closed tight. Sealed. Then the hatch is opened and the dock here is flooded just enough for the submarine to float out into the sea. The door closes, the dock drains, then the steel door opens again and all is back to normal. Clever, no?'

'Clever,' agreed Oak.

Cate looked at the remnants of seawater still drying on the walls of the dock.

'It went out not long ago?' she asked.

José shook his head. 'No, Tass has not taken it out since he has been here in Antibes.'

Well, someone has used it, thought Cate. *In the last day or so by the look of it and, if it wasn't Tass taking a pleasure trip, that must mean that the submarine was being used for something more businesslike. Moving animals around for example.*

She seized her chance. 'José,' she said loudly, making sure that the children could hear her. 'José, I know I shouldn't ask, but would it be, in any way at all, possible for us to have a teeny little look in the submarine. Wouldn't that be great, children?'

'Yes, yes, please, please let's have a look, please,' chorused Oak and the twins. To Cate's secret delight, little Willow dropped down onto her knees in a parody of begging. Cate saw José hesitate, his eyes swivelling from the children to the fat man who was sitting watching them from his position back along the corridor.

'I will ask,' said José, weakening. 'Wait here.'

He walked back to the guard and for a few minutes she could hear the soft murmur of voices. Then he went over to a telephone that was set into the wall. He dialled a number and waited patiently but clearly there was no answer.

'These phones,' he grumbled. 'They never work down here in the submarine bay. The walkie talkies are the same. It's a waste of time trying.' José came to a decision. 'OK, kids,' he said good-naturedly. 'Just a quick look. But be very, very careful OK and no touching the controls.'

Cate thought fast. She had to get into the secret room and to do that she had to get past the guard. She looked back, sizing him up. He was unfit, that was for sure. But taking him on was not the answer. He'd just call for help and that would be that. No, there had to be another way.

Excitedly, the children filed onto the submarine, Oak leading the way, José and Cate bringing up the rear. The inside was disappointing, rather like a small bus, but with only a few forward facing seats and with a large cargo area. The interior was immaculate, smelling strongly of bleach and disinfectant as if it had just been washed out. Plenty of room for animals, but if there had been any in there recently, there was no sign of them now.

The younger children charged up and down the aisle climbing on the seats and trying to jump up and touch the low cream ceilings.

But the real excitement lay up at the front of the submarine where the controls were flashing and bleeping like something from an old-fashioned space movie.

'Whatever you do, don't press that red button.' José pointed to a large round knob that lay just above the eye line of a mesmerised Oak. 'That will start the engines and the process of shutting the hatches between us and the rest of the ship.'

He turned his back and went towards the rear of the submarine where some of the children were amusing themselves by trying to spot fish in the dark murky waters. Cate, with Beech toddling alongside quietly, headed into the cramped control room.

Cate gave Beech a quick cuddle, took a deep breath and hit the red button. As the engines roared to life, she shouted to a startled José, 'Don't worry, I'll go for help!' She sprinted off the submarine, through the already closing shutter into the corridor.

The guard looked startled.

'One of the kids hit the red button,' panted Cate.

'It'll be OK.' The fat man was in no hurry to move. 'As long as the submarine isn't running, the shutter will reach the bottom and then go back up again automatically.'

No! thought Cate. *What do I have to do to get you out of your seat?*

'The engines have started and water is coming in,' she tried again. 'José really needs your help.'

This time the guard sprang to his feet and as fast as his bulk would let him hurried towards the submarine bay.

Cate already had the memory stick in her hand. By the time the guard was ducking under the nearly closed shutters, she had slotted it into the USB port at the base of the computer.

She clicked around the screen, searching frantically for a security file. It wasn't on the desktop, nor was it in favourites and now Cate was starting to panic. Suddenly she had a brainwave – she went into the hard drive, searched for *Security* and there in front of her was a folder entitled *Room Entry*. She looked up. The doors were still closing slowly, now way too low for either José or the guard to make it back. She reckoned she had around two minutes before the shutters rose up far enough to let the trapped men back into her side of the door.

She right clicked on the folder and selected the copy option. The file began to download to the data card, agonisingly slowly at first and then gathering speed. The screen showed seventy seconds left to go before the download was completed. The steel door had reached the bottom and now was bouncing gently as it settled. Fifty seconds to go – the shutters were beginning to clatter at the start of their upward climb. Thirty seconds – Cate's hands were shaking as they hovered over the mouse waiting to click back to the original page. Twenty seconds – she could see the feet of the children. Ten seconds – the men were bending down ready to come through – hurry, hurry! The computer gave out a soft bleep – *Copy complete.* Cate removed the stick and just as the first of the children came bursting back towards her shouting with excitement at their adventure, she managed to clear the screen. By the time the two men were able to get under the door she was halfway down the corridor, kneeling down, cuddling the children and wearing her best distraught look.

The guard lumbered towards her, glaring at her, angry at everyone. 'What a shambles,' he was shouting. 'Whose stupid idea was it to let these kids come down here?'

'Tass,' said Cate, over the noise of the children. 'He loves these kids.'

The guard went quiet. José looked pale with shock and stood silently, so Cate took charge. 'You know what?' she said.

'I think we should all forget this ever happened. We're all safe, no harm done. Right, kids?'

The children nodded solemnly.

José and the guard looked at each other. José was still shaking. 'You think?' he said hopefully.

The guard shrugged. Cate could see the battle was won.

'Personally,' said Cate, forcing tears into her eyes. 'I need this job. I really do.'

'OK,' said José, patting her on the shoulder. 'Don't cry, Cate. We agree. Let's forget all about it. But believe me, I am never ever volunteering to show kids around again.'

Halfway there, thought Cate triumphantly, as they climbed into the lift and rose back up to the world of luxury and sunshine. Now she just had to get around the hand scan.

After lunch, Cate suggested the children watch a movie. They finally all agreed on *Alvin and the Chipmunks*.

'Any news from Mikey?' asked Cate casually, as José handed her a freshly squeezed apple juice.

'Ahh.' José sounded exasperated. 'They are not coming back until late tonight. They have got rid of the paparazzi but now Tass and Nancy have taken Mikey and Ahmed over to Cannes where some friends are having a film premiere at the Ritz Carlton.'

'What about the other guys? The bodyguards who went with them.'

'They have been left on the *Catwalk II* for now at least. To frighten off the paparazzi. But don't worry yourself, Cate. You are safe here with José!'

He grinned benevolently at her and she smiled back. He

really seemed to be a nice man and she hoped against hope he wasn't mixed up with the bad guys.

The film began and the children were soon glued to the screen. Cate gave them five minutes to get properly hooked and then, in a whisper, leant over and asked Oak for his phone.

Oak slid it carefully under his armrest and onto Cate's lap. She took it from him and, under cover of the half light, slipped off the back, removed his sim card and data card and put her own sim and data card from the IMIA data stick in. It took a few minutes to boot up and then, keeping the phone down below the seat, she began to text Arthur.

Am sending security files to your server. Please bypass need for hand recognition to access Room One within an hour. PS DO NOT CALL. She pressed send. Thank God it was Saturday. With any luck Arthur would be at home.

Then, using one hand and pretending to eat popcorn with the other, she sent the files. She held her breath. Would the phone be able to cope with sending the huge volume of information she had downloaded from the security computer or would it simply crash?

The upload bar appeared but it grew slowly, painfully slowly, and Cate knew that the longer it took to transmit, the more chance there was of the signal being picked up and intercepted by the huge bank of technology on board the yacht.

A minute later, the file was still transmitting and Cate found herself craning her neck, half expecting shadowy figures to come piling in through the velvet curtains to grab the phone from her sweaty hand. Finally the phone screen changed. *File uploaded.*

Cate checked her watch. She would feel much safer if the job was done and downloaded under cover of the film but she had an awful feeling that she had set her brother an almost impossible task. She texted him. *Need it back before three p.m. otherwise too late. Please respond asap.*

She sat back. There was nothing more she could do now. She glanced along the line of the enraptured children, their hands automatically dipping in and out of the popcorn buckets, then tried again to watch the film but the chirruping chipmunks and the gooning around of the human co-stars made her head spin.

Then to her utter relief, the phone vibrated in her hand. *Blimey, you don't want much*, Arthur had texted. *Am working on it as we speak. Seen worse. Three p.m. fine.*

Cate settled back in her seat. Suddenly the film seemed to be very funny after all. Just as the credits were rolling Arthur's file finished downloading to the data card. *Good old Arthur*, thought Cate. *He always comes through.*

At six o'clock there was a shift changeover. The first Cate knew of it was when she heard a clatter of steps on the metal spiral staircase that came up from the bottom floor to the staff mess on the lower ground floor. Worn out by another long swim in the pool, the younger children were asleep and the older three were watching TV in a guest bedroom.

Cate was in the mess room having a few quiet minutes to herself, drinking tea and trying to work out just how to get back into the secure area and, more importantly, back to the security station without raising any suspicion.

Suddenly she spotted the fat guard sitting on his own with a large tin of biscuits. He was concentrating hard, working his way methodically through the chocolate ones and discarding the plain.

'Hi,' said Cate, walking over to him and putting on her friendliest face. 'I'm so glad I caught you.' He looked at her warily, still chewing, crumbs on either side of his mouth. 'You're not going to believe it but little Beech must've left her favourite teddy bear behind in the submarine bay. Could you possibly — '

'No way.' Mr Lardy suddenly came to life. 'I've finished for the day, clocked off. Done. I'm just waiting for the boat to come and get me and I'm off for the rest of the weekend.'

Cate looked disappointed. 'But little Beech was so desperate – distraught.' Cate paused. 'Awful thing to see a little one cry herself to sleep. Have you got kids?'

'Nope.' The man sounded bored. He had resumed his chewing and was rummaging in the biscuit tin for more of his favourites.

'I've spent hours looking for it,' Cate persevered. 'The only place I haven't checked is the submarine bay. It has to be there.' She shook her head, looking worried. 'I don't know how I'm going to explain it to Nancy and Tass. And of course, Beech would be Tass's favourite kid.'

The man grunted. That hit home. He finally turned to look at Cate. 'It's your problem, not mine. I'm not missing my boat for any two-year-old or a teddy bear. But I'll radio downstairs and ask them if they'll let you back into the secure area to have a look.' He turned away and reached for a walkie talkie that was wedged into his chest pocket. 'Kids,' he snorted. 'Shouldn't be allowed anywhere near a boat.'

'Thanks,' said Cate to the back of his head. 'Thanks a million.' Cate pressed the call button for the lift. 'You'll go straight to heaven you will.' Probably a McDonald's in his case Cate thought and then checked herself. *Not very kind, Cate.* This man had just done her a huge favour and here she was dissing him in return. She was getting quite catty in her old age. If she wasn't careful she would end up as bitchy as Lulu.

Lulu. As Cate got into the lift she had to stop herself from shouting out. Of course, Lulu. What had Nancy said? She said Lulu had introduced them. Lulu knew loads of people.

Cate pressed the button for the bottom floor and forced herself to concentrate. It was Lulu who looked after every single detail of Nancy's affairs, even down to how much money the supermodel had in her bank account at any one time.

Everywhere Nancy went Lulu was there at her shoulder, guiding her, advising her, chastising her, even introducing her to boyfriends. *Playing her*, thought Cate grimly, *like a violin*. Lulu would have been with Nancy in Africa, in Asia, in Mexico. God, Lulu probably set the trips up, booked the flights and even arranged the adoptions. Nancy just had to turn up and look beautiful.

It all made perfect sense. If Nancy had something to hide, why had she openly told Cate that she and Tass were working together on an environmental project? And Nancy showed no sign of knowing the professor was dead.

That was another thing. Cate had seen Nancy with her children. Nancy wasn't ruthless. Nancy was from a loving

186

family who gave her a happy childhood and she, at least, was making a good attempt at being a caring mother herself. But Lulu, now there was definitely something scary about her, something very cold and ruthless.

Cate shook her head, amazed that neither she nor the IMIA had seen it before. It wasn't Nancy who was the link to all these missing animals, she was sure, it was Lulu. Lulu, Bill and, unless his boat was being visited by Bill without his knowlege, almost certainly Tass as well.

The doors opened and immediately one of the guards was coming towards her, his sunburnt face expressionless. 'You Cate?'

She nodded.

'We were told you were coming.'

They walked silently down towards the secure area, past the banks of computer monitors and the security footage. At the double door he punched in the security code which, Cate noticed, hadn't changed from that morning and, as they opened, nodded to a ginger-haired man sitting at the guard's desk. 'Here's the nanny. Come to look for the teddy bear. Don't be long.'

The door shut and Cate and the guard looked at each other. He nodded at her, fiddled with the computer mouse and the steel shutters at the end of the corridor began to rise again.

'You'll be all right?' the man spoke with a drawling Southern American accent. 'I'll stay here.'

Blimey, thought Cate. *What is it with these guys? Are they superglued to their seats?* But she nodded her agreement and walked down the corridor, waiting patiently whilst the shutters clattered upwards.

She walked slowly into the dark bay, the submarine looking even more sinister, wallowing like some giant primeval animal half in and half out of the water. She almost expected the sub's giant nose to open like a set of jaws and lunge towards her. *Pull yourself together*, she thought.

She walked noisily onto the gangplank and into the submarine control room, pulled a small stripy teddy bear from her bag and pushed it under the bank of dials, waited a few seconds and then came back to the doors.

'I can't get the lights on,' she called. 'I can't see anything – would you mind?'

Grunting, the man rose to his feet. He was very tall, Cate noticed, with a face that looked as if it had seen a few punch-ups. He wandered down the corridor and boarded the submarine, Cate following in his wake. Flashing his torch, he felt around the base of the submarine and flicked a switch.

'I feel sick,' said Cate suddenly, as light flooded the submarine. 'I'm going to be sick. I think I'm claustrophobic.' The guard looked alarmed as Cate leant against the submarine wall. 'Do you have a loo?'

He nodded. 'Back up near my desk.'

'Sorry, gotta go. Can you look for the bear? It's stripy.' Hand over her mouth, she ran back across the gangplank and out from the bay.

As she entered the corridor she noticed the guard head back down into the submarine to carry on the search for the bear. He was behaving himself beautifully, Cate thought. She ran to the computer. The screen was showing the same options as it had before, she clicked onto *Door Two* and then chose the *Close* option. Immediately the shutters began to move downwards. Now she had to pray that the guard would not hear them until it was too late.

She stood by the screen holding her breath. Fifteen seconds passed and the shutters were almost down when she heard a shout from the guard. 'Hey!' he said. 'What's going on?' She saw his hands scramble at the bottom of the shutters, trying desperately to pull them up. He crouched down, clearly considering whether he had enough time to slip under them. But it was too late. With a defiant clang, the shutters were down. Cate turned back to the screen, clicked on options again. *Seal Room* or *Open Door* came up. 'The former I think,' Cate said to herself.

Within seconds she had the data stick back in the computer. *Here goes nothing*, she thought as she opened Arthur's file and his override program started running. The security guard banged on the shutter doors as the file downloaded into the computer. Cate flicked back to the original screen with its *Room One* and *Room Two*. Her hands shaking, Cate clicked the first option. *Please*, she thought, *please let it work*.

There was a soft click from the door opposite. She grabbed the data stick and, hardly daring to believe what she was hearing, Cate went over and pushed at the door gently, sending a silent thank you to Arthur as she did so. It swung into a dark space and Cate fiddled around for the light switch, blinking as light flooded the room.

The room was tiny, barely three metres by two metres with a low ceiling. It smelt stuffy and stale, the cork tiles underfoot loose and ragged. It was furnished with a small, plain desk, a grey plastic chair and white-fronted cupboards which ran at waist height around the room.

To Cate's disappointment there was no sign of a phone, a computer screen and certainly not a laptop. Cate went quickly through the cupboards, checking with her hands back into the furthest corners, but they were empty.

She looked at her watch desperately. A minute gone already. What was this room for? Why all the fuss? There must be something here.

She got down on her hands and knees and worked her way methodically across the floor, rapping with her knuckles as she went. Nothing. The floor was solid, concrete, probably thick. But there was nowhere else to look so, with her knuckles already sore, she kept trying, rapping right down to the far end of the room where the light was dim. Then, when she had all but reached the far wall she heard the sound change from dull to echoey. The floor had suddenly become hollow.

Cate scrabbled at a loose tile and it came away easily. Under it was a small wood cover which lifted up as she pushed down at one end. There in front of her was the blue laptop!

Cate caught her breath in a sob of relief. She opened it up and pressed the on button, praying that the batteries still had life in them. The screen lit up in front of her, the wallpaper a beautiful photograph of a mountain gorilla. She inserted her datastick and then began a frantic search copying recently viewed and amended files.

Cate waited for the files to copy, trying hard to contain her terror as the time ticked slowly by. As she did so her hand brushed against what seemed to be a light switch; suddenly there was a smooth *whoosh* and a door-sized piece of wall moved slowly to one side.

Cate stared at it, amazed. At first she thought it was just a hole and then realised she was looking at a glass door. She walked towards it, peered through it and nearly screamed. There, stretching out in front of her, was a row of cages of varying sizes and shapes. And each one contained an animal. Exactly the same animals she had seen in that awful film just a few days ago. She had found them at last.

CHAPTER 15

Cate clapped her hand to her mouth. She felt sick with shock, could hear blood rushing through her ears and, as she looked down, she saw her hands were shaking. She hadn't expected this, not here, not now.

She desperately wanted to rush in and free the animals and whisk them up to the fresh air and sunlight just a few tantalising metres above them. But she knew that was impossible.

At least they weren't in squalor. Cate had expected that, when she found the animals, they would be in an awful condition. But although these animals looked miserable, physically they were in good shape; clean and well fed.

She hated to leave them in their misery for even a few hours longer, but she had to. She pressed the switch and watched sadly as the door whirred back into place. Cate felt as if she was torturing them too, as cruel and as wicked as the people who had wrenched them from their natural habitat and brought them into this terrible place. She forced herself back to the laptop, to concentrate on the task in hand. 'Nearly there,' she consoled herself. 'Nearly there.'

Finally the download was complete. Cate slipped the laptop back into its hiding place, switched off the light and pulled the door closed behind her. It locked fast.

She let out a huge gasp of air and looked at her watch. The whole thing had taken less than three minutes. She ran back down to the shutters. The guard had stopped banging now.

'Hello?' she called out, sounding panic-stricken. 'Hello? Where are you? Are you OK?'

'I'm stuck, you goddamn stupid girl.' Despite his obvious annoyance the guard sounded relieved. 'The shutter system has stuck. Where the hell have you been all this time? Didn't you hear me shouting?'

'Oh, I've been so sick,' Cate whined. 'I've been in that loo for ages. It must have been something I ate. Shall I get help?'

'The computer must have frozen. Do you know how to work computers?'

'I can try,' said Cate meekly. 'What shall I do?'

The guard sounded exasperated as he gave her the instructions. As Cate went to the computer and opened the submarine door, she took some deep breaths, trying to calm herself down.

'About goddamn time too.' The guard snorted angrily as his lower body came gradually into view. 'What a mess.' In his left hand he held a small green and white bear.

'Stripy!' said Cate, rushing towards him. 'You found Stripy! Thank you so, so much.'

The guard handed the bear over and gestured impatiently towards the door. 'I'm not in the mood, kid,' he said. 'Get going and take your stupid bear with you. And don't come back.'

It was dark by the time Mikey and Ahmed came to pick them up. As the powerboat pulled into the mini harbour, Cate and the children were already waiting for them on the boardwalk.

Now all she had to do was get back to the *Catwalk II* and brief Marcus and it would all be over. Surely the IMIA would make their move now.

Cate, who felt as if she had been waiting for days rather than just a few hours to get off the boat, hustled them quickly onboard.

'You're keen,' said Mikey, gesturing to the pilot to start the engine.

'The kids are tired and so am I,' said Cate as the boat reversed back into the sea.

When she got back, Marcus was nowhere to be seen. Cate was desperate to tell him what she had found and sent him a text. She needed him to call her urgently.

Returning to her cabin, Cate was so tired that it was all she could do to fire up her computer and send Arthur the information she had grabbed from the blue laptop. She had got as far as she could on her own, now she needed someone else to help her to put the final pieces of the puzzle together.

The next thing Cate knew it was morning, the sunlight was streaming through her porthole and her phone was vibrating on her bedside table. It was Arthur, his voice shaking with excitement.

'Cate, Cate, are you awake?' Arthur was having trouble getting his words out. 'I've been through the files you sent me. It's unbelievable, horrible, obscene. No wonder they were prepared to kill. Cate, whatever it takes, you have to stop it.'

'Do you need some shopping done, Marcus?' Cate had just arrived up on deck and found Marcus in the galley working on breakfast. He was waiting for her, she knew, from the text he had sent to her sometime during the night when she was too deeply asleep to hear it. It was time to set up what she hoped would be the final meeting with the IMIA.

'Wendy is looking after the kids this morning and I thought I would have a break, go for a run. I was thinking you might need something from the fish shop?' Cate asked.

Marcus looked sharply at her as she leant against the door frame of the galley. Behind her, Bill was pottering around in the navigation bay, well within earshot of their conversation.

'Actually, I was going to nip up there myself this morning,' he said casually. 'About nine-ish. See what's come in on the overnight boats. Thanks for the offer but I fancy a walk anyway.' He winked at her and mouthed, 'See you later.'

Cate nodded and turned without answering as Wendy appeared from the salon carrying dirty breakfast bowls.

'Well done, yesterday, I hear the kids had a great time,' she said kindly. 'And you'll be very glad to know that the new nanny will arrive today. You're off the hook with the kids.'

Cate seized her chance. 'In that case, Wendy, do you mind if I have a break now for a couple of hours, please? Just get off the boat, have a run, maybe a coffee?'

'No worries, Cate. You can have until lunchtime.'

Ten minutes later Cate, dressed in her running gear, headed into town. Antibes was slowly waking up from its Saturday night to another still morning.

It's all so beautiful, Cate thought, as she ran to the fish shop. *Maybe soon, when all this is over, I can begin to properly enjoy it. Maybe even with Michel.*

She stood for a short while outside the fish shop, watching as the streets gradually became busier, fantasising that Michel might walk past her and then panicking in case he did. She was almost relieved when she spotted Marcus making his way up towards her from the bottom of the hill. She took a deep breath. Time to get to work.

She headed into the alleyway and climbed up the rusty iron stairway once more. As she reached the top of the steps, Marcus was behind her, pushing at the door to let her in ahead of him.

'Marcus, it would be best if I could speak to all of you,' Cate shouted above the rattle as the ancient lift swayed down into the depths of the caves. 'You, Piot and Henri. Would that be OK? Are they there?'

Marcus nodded.

The lift doors wrenched themselves open and Cate and Marcus stepped out into the cool air. Up ahead of them were Henri and Piot.

Piot put his hand on her shoulder. 'Good to see you again, Cate. I hear you've been amazing.'

Cate gave him a grateful smile and dumped her rucksack onto the desk. 'We need to get Arthur on the line,' she said.

The room fell silent. Cate pulled out her laptop and set it on the table. She sat down next to it and gazed at the faces of the adults watching her. She knew they were waiting for her to talk but she couldn't tell the whole story alone.

'I need internet access,' she said flatly.

Henri waved to a man poring over a computer screen on the other side of the room and, handing him the laptop, whispered some instructions to him.

'The conference line will be set up in five,' he told the group. 'In the meantime, Cate, can you bring us all up to date?'

'Andrei was right,' Cate began. 'Everything we needed to know was on *The Good Times*.'

None of the adults moved a muscle, watching her closely as she spoke. 'Down at the bottom of the yacht, right at the front is a secret room. It is so secret hardly anyone on the boat even knows about it. The animals you have been looking for are in there, crammed into that room, in the darkness. According to Professor Mantanini's files, they are the end results of two years of experimentation and will shortly be paraded, by Tass Taplinski, in front of the world's media as the pioneers of a great age of rare animal survival.'

No one said a word.

'Those animals were stolen to order, brought to Tendo and then taken on to St Tropez,' Cate continued, 'to that lab, where Professor Mantanini was waiting for them. He'd spent months, years, working on God knows how many similar animals, trying to perfect his research and then discarding those

197

beautiful creatures when he had finished with them.' Her voice trailed off and for a moment she struggled to continue.

'That was what he was doing in his lab. Those poor animals were brought there all that way from their homeland, to be experimented on.

'Tass wasn't stealing them,' Cate continued. 'Not in his mind, anyway. They were essential for vital experimentation. He wanted to clone them, you see. Clone them so that they would no longer be endangered. Well, that was the original plan. And that's what he told Nancy, who believed him. Why shouldn't she? She is madly in love with him and she thought he was doing her a massive favour by putting money into her animal charity. But really it was the other way around. Nancy was invaluable to Tass. Tass would never have been able to walk into reserves like that and gain access to so many animals. But, with her charity work, she could get easy access to the animal reserves and no one would ever suspect her of being involved with stealing the animals.'

'But how did they get the animals out?' Henri asked.

'Good old-fashioned bribery,' said Cate. 'Arthur found the accounts. Tass channelled the money via Nancy's charities through various officials worldwide in charge of animal welfare. Half the money went to him to make sure the animals passed safely through their country and out to the nearest docks. The other half, well it went to an account in the name of Louisa Katerina Sobieski.'

'Lulu,' Marcus said flatly. 'Of course, it was Lulu.'

'She was the missing link, the paymaster,' agreed Cate. 'She accompanied Nancy around the world, setting up the trips, organising the publicity stunts, even writing Nancy's soppy speeches.

'And all the time she was using that access to get to those precious animals. She probably handed over wodges of cash to some poor sap on the animal reserve in return for a baby animal for just a week or so. Or perhaps she convinced them it was for a secret photo shoot, or for a fundraising publicity stunt. Either way it probably seemed innocent enough and, when the animals weren't returned, the staff were always too frightened to own up. I bet Lulu can be nasty when she's crossed.'

'Wow,' said Piot. He looked shocked. 'Good work, Cate.'

'Actually, it doesn't make sense at all,' Henri broke in tersely. 'Tass isn't the first person to try to clone endangered animals, and he won't be the last. There are always dozens of backers for these sorts of schemes so, even if people knew what he was doing, it would hardly raise eyebrows let alone cause shockwaves. There wasn't really the need for such secrecy, let alone the thuggery and the killings. No, it's not enough. There is something else going on here, something that doesn't fit in with what Cate is telling us.'

'You're dead right.' Cate turned to him. 'That's exactly what I couldn't work out, either. Arthur will tell you better than I can,' she continued quietly. 'It was all on the laptop, but it was Arthur who worked out what it meant.'

As if on cue, the computer technician came over to the group. 'We're ready to go online now,' he said to no one in particular. 'Give me the IP address and we'll be good to go.'

'I'll do it,' said Cate. She walked over to his computer and

199

typed in Arthur's details. Within a few seconds Arthur's face was up on the large screen above them, his disembodied voice sounding even more child-like as it wafted through the speakers and up into the cavernous ceiling.

'Hi, Cate,' he said nervously. 'Hi . . . everyone.'

There was a murmured 'hello' from the grown-ups standing below him.

'Arthur,' said Cate, walking over to the screen and standing as close to it as she could. 'Arthur, tell them what Professor Mantanini was really up to. Tell them why he had to die.'

'I couldn't believe it at first.' Arthur was speaking in a low voice and the others, further away than Cate, had to strain to hear him. 'It seemed so awful that I thought I must have got it wrong. But I went through it over and over last night. There's no mistake.' He paused.

'Go on, Arthur,' said Cate.

'It wasn't actually that difficult to find,' said Arthur. 'You did all the sweatwork getting hold of the files, sis. But anyway, like you asked, I started searching through the files and there was a series of emails that told the story.

'The professor wasn't cloning, well, not any more. It seems that, when he was working as a cloning expert, his research produced an added bonus. He realised that he could manipulate the DNA of animals to stop them getting old.'

Arthur stopped for a minute, his face pale and sad, trying to compose himself. 'He'd found out how to essentially switch off the ageing gene of mammals,' said Arthur. 'That's why he started using very young animals, creatures who were still growing fast. It was easier to tell if they had stopped growing.

The animals Cate found are two years old but physically they are no older than six months.

'There were a few problems as he developed his work.' Arthur's voice dropped to a whisper. 'He sent emails to Tass telling him about animals becoming horribly disfigured with skin blisters and muscle wasting. Others ended up unable to see or even breathe properly. One or two aged overnight and a couple went properly mad. But then the professor would simply destroy them and put in an order to Tass and his gang for more animals. Then one day it all came together. As soon as the animals showed they weren't ageing, and research was finalised, the professor became expendable.'

Arthur paused watching the reaction from the adults around him. Did they believe him? Did they even understand him?

The men were staring dumbstruck at the screen. Finally Piot broke the silence. 'I don't get it,' he said honestly. 'Can you please run it by me one more time?'

'He was creating animals that would never grow old,' said Henri slowly. 'He was deliberately removing from them any ability to age, to grow up to adulthood, to reproduce, to grow old, to die.'

There was a stunned silence as the adults digested the awful truth.

'God,' said Marcus. 'No wonder Tass wanted to keep it quiet. Something like that would have the scientific world in uproar. You're right, Arthur.' He turned to the boy. 'The thought of something as powerful as that in the wrong hands is utterly terrifying. But unethical and immoral as it may be, there would always be someone who would want a piece of it.'

'That's right,' said Cate. 'Sometime in the next few months, Tass was going to parade the animals in front of the world's media – and not just any animals, endangered animals, which would get even more attention. He wouldn't tell them about the thefts, of course, or how many animals had died terrified and in agony, in the process – it would ruin what reputation he'd built. So he had to bury the truth. Take the professor's files and make sure the professor could never reveal the lengths Tass went to.'

'But why?' Henri was impatient. 'Tass has all the money he could ever need. He wouldn't need to sell the research.'

Cate turned to him. 'He wanted his dad to be proud of him,' she said quietly. 'That's what I think. That was all. He wanted his dad's approval.'

Henri coughed. 'Er, Cate, what has that got to do with those animals?'

'Don't you see, Henri?' Cate said. 'It has everything to do with it. I thought about what Nancy had told me. About Tass having his dad on his case all the time. I thought of how he must feel, how badly he must have wanted his dad's respect. He knew he had to do something amazing, something incredible. He had to literally save the world. Or, in his case, he decided he had to save the animal world, but ended up with something far more ground-breaking.'

Marcus smiled and shook his head. 'Of course,' he said. 'That makes sense. Why else would he risk so much? But how exactly was saving endangered animals going to get his dad to bring out the cheerleaders?'

'It would have given him the success he craved, money and power beyond his wildest dreams,' said Piot slowly. 'It would have made his dad sit up and take notice.'

'We need those animals alive,' Henri said firmly, dragging them back to the practicalities. 'That would provide the definite proof. We need to storm the boat, mount a rescue operation, arrest the crew.'

'You can try.' Arthur spoke again, high above them. 'But I doubt you'll succeed. A small army wouldn't be able to storm that boat, and in any case, they'd see you coming a mile off.'

'He's right,' Marcus said. 'Tass has got powerboats and that damn submarine. Those animals would be gone long before we even got onboard. We have to do this by stealth. Somehow, someone needs to get onto the yacht and disarm the defences to give us any chance of a happy ending.'

This time the silence seemed to last forever. Three pairs of eyes swivelled towards Cate.

'Cate?' said Henri finally, sounding rather as if he was asking her if she fancied a cup of tea. 'Cate, how do you feel about one more trip out to *The Good Times*? Sooner rather than later.'

CHAPTER 16

'Ooowww.' Nancy's screams reverberated around *Catwalk II*. 'God, what are you – some kind of sadist?'

Jules tugged hard at the waxing strips that were plastered on her legs.

Cate, who was giving the children lunch in the salon, could hardly contain her giggles.

'What's Jules doing to Mummy?' asked Willow as she fed her bear some smoked salmon.

'They're making her beautiful,' said Oak, not looking up from his book. 'By ripping her hair out.'

'Oh,' said Ash. 'Yuck.'

Cate looked down at her phone, checking for texts but there were none. In truth she didn't expect any. After all, if you pulled out of a first date just a few hours before it was due to take place you couldn't exactly expect the bloke to be delighted.

I wouldn't be surprised if he never wanted to see me again, Cate thought glumly, as she remembered his gorgeous eyes and charming smile.

She hadn't heard back from Arthur either, not after the two of them had had their worst ever row.

He had been furious with her, frightened too, she knew. He had even shouted at Marcus and Henri, told them they were risking Cate's life, and she was shaken by the depth of his fear.

'These are really dangerous people,' he kept saying. 'They killed the professor, they'll kill you if they catch you.'

Piot too had been on Arthur's side. 'Cate is a child,' he said to Henri. 'What kind of people are we to send a child back into danger? What if something terrible happens to her?'

Henri had snorted then. 'Cate is not a child. She's a, a . . .' he searched for the right words. 'She's a fighter, a warrior, a natural-born spy. She's perfect for this job. If anyone else goes onboard that ship the alarm will be raised and the game will be over. Cate knows the boat already, and she has the best chance of getting access without raising suspicion. No one else has a hope of rescuing those animals without her help and you know it.'

The arguments had ceased then, Marcus and Henri nodding their agreement, Piot walking away in disgust. Even Arthur was finally quiet, wishing his sister a terse and strained goodbye.

'Well,' Henri had said briskly, as Arthur had vanished from the screen in front of them. 'That's settled. Cate, liaise with Marcus. Let him know what you need and when you need it. The entire resources of the department are at your disposal. Good luck.'

'Has anyone spotted Bill lately?' It was Wendy, walking through the cabin with a pile of towels in her hand, bringing Cate back to the present. 'I haven't seen him since this morning.'

'Isn't he down in the mess?' asked Cate. 'Or have you tried the engine room?'

'Nah, looked down there,' said Wendy. 'Perhaps he's gone somewhere with Lulu. I haven't seen her all day either. Well, if you see him, tell him I need him. Nancy wanted to plan a trip down to Sardinia this week.'

Just then, the door to Nancy's cabin burst open and the supermodel, her waxing ordeal clearly over, danced out wearing a metallic gold bikini and a pair of oversized sunglasses. She was trailed by a rather rotund girl wearing a pair of jeans and a billowing kaftan top which made her look even larger. The new nanny, Cate presumed.

'Darlings!' said Nancy, as the children looked up, astonished at her sudden appearance. 'Tonight we are going to be a family, a proper family.'

The children looked blankly at her.

'Tass and me, and all of you beautiful, gorgeous kids. We're spending a lovely evening in together, eating pizza and watching Disney films down here in the salon. We're going to make up a bed on the floor with heaps of duvets and eat popcorn. Won't that be fabulous?'

The younger children beamed happily, caught up in the excitement.

Oak looked less pleased. 'Does Tass have to be there?' he said, looking up at his mother. 'Wouldn't it be better if it was just us lot? You know he doesn't like us anyway.'

'Oak, that's so not true!' Nancy sounded outraged. 'This was all his idea.'

'Yeah, right,' murmured Oak.

That afternoon, Cate, spotting that Suki, the new nanny, was already looking stressed, volunteered to take the children to the beach near the harbour. It was crowded with families enjoying the bright sunny Sunday afternoon.

A little white dog ran in and out of the sea, barking at the waves, and a delighted Elm and Ash threw sticks for it into the water. Beech lay asleep, covered up by towels and, at the far end of the scimitar-shaped beach, Oak and Willow were clambering happily together over heaped up piles of rocks.

Cate sat hugging her knees, absorbing the happiness around her, trying not to think of the danger that was to come. She shook her head and crossed her finger grimly. *This time tomorrow*, she promised herself, *it will be all over*.

By seven o'clock that evening, the children were bathed, changed into their pyjamas and already lying heaped over quilts and pillows that had been strewn across the salon floor in front of the TV.

Nancy was with them on the floor whilst Tass sat stiffly on one of the huge cream sofas, fiddling with the remote control. Cate waved goodnight to the children and went to see Marcus who was in the galley preparing the pizzas.

'Let's run through the plan to get you onboard one more time,' said Marcus, shutting the door quietly behind her. 'We don't want any needless mistakes.'

Ten minutes later, as dusk was falling, Cate headed off the

boat onto the still warm pontoon. The lights from the boats glowed and flickered around her, and she could hear music from a yacht behind *Catwalk II* and the sound of people laughing. Cate was wearing her black leggings, a black jogging top and black trainers, her hair tucked into a dark scarf she had borrowed from Nancy's collection. In her rucksack she was carrying her phone, a Swiss Army knife, a powerful miniature torch, the survival kit and this time, after much deliberation with Marcus, the gun.

The red powerboat belonging to *The Good Times* was tied up to a small seaweed-encrusted post close to *Catwalk II* awaiting Tass and his bodyguards for their return trip to *The Good Times*. It was an easy job for Cate to step down into it as it bobbed around gently in the marina. She held her breath, waiting for an alarm or something to go off. But everything stayed quiet. Only the chirp of the cicadas from the park over the road disturbed the peaceful early evening air.

She leant back over the pontoon and scraped up some of the sea mud left in between the slats by the high tide and smeared it over her bare arms and her face then checked her watch. Three minutes to eight. Any time now.

On the dot of eight, she heard the first *thud, thud* of the helicopters as they flew in formation out from the hills behind the town and swooped low over the harbour, heading out to sea to hover over where *The Good Times* was moored. A few seconds later, Cate watched as huge flares lit up the sky, fired as a first warning by *The Good Times*' powerful anti-aircraft system. Marcus hadn't let her down.

As arranged, the helicopters were holding their position and

Cate heard a terrifyingly loud crackle as *The Good Times* fired electricity into the air to disrupt the helicopters' flight. She watched the mayhem for a few seconds longer and then opened the hatch in the deck which housed the powerful inboard engine. There was just enough room for her to squeeze safely alongside the metal block without danger of being trapped on the propeller. Good old Marcus. He had done his research well. Cate slipped in and pulled the hatch over her head. A minute later, she heard the sound of running footsteps on the pontoon.

Tass was onto the boat first, she could tell by his lighter tread. Then two heavier sets of footsteps: Ahmed and Mikey. They were cursing and shouting, struggling to get the ropes undone and the engine started. Cate pulled out a pair of earplugs from her pocket and shoved them into her ears just as the engine roared to life beside her. As the boat pounded at top speed over the waves, Cate hugged herself in the dark, her heart pounding and her mouth dry. She concentrated hard. For the next few hours she had to be razor sharp and she couldn't let the fear of what she was headed into overpower her mind.

As the boat slowed to a stop, Cate pulled her earplugs out. She could hear Tass's men shouting, trying to be heard over the clatter of the choppers, the whizzing of the flares being dropped from the helicopters and, even more ominously, the rattle of bullets.

It's chaos, thought Cate. Her adrenalin was pumping and she was no longer scared, her mind cool and focused. *It's time to get to work*.

She looked down at the black trainers she was wearing,

remembering what Marcus had told her as he handed them to her earlier that day.

'Look at the soles,' he had told her.

Cate had turned the shoes over and stared at the bottom of them. They looked completely normal. She pushed and prodded. Nothing.

'Twist them, Super Spy!' said Marcus, sounding exasperated.

'Ooops, sorry,' said Cate, grabbing one of the studs and turning it. It came away almost instantly, leaving a hollow space beneath it. Nestled into it was a shiny black vial. Cate went to touch it.

'Don't,' said Marcus sharply. 'It's carborane acid – a superacid hundreds of times more powerful than, say, sulphuric acid. There's a vial in every stud and they are perfectly safely packaged there. Only take them out when you are about to use them.'

'Once the vial is opened the superacid becomes active within sixty seconds. You understand? Once that process is started there is no turning back.'

Cate stared at him, enthralled and repulsed at the same time. 'You mean I'm walking around with a highly destructive acid in my shoes?'

Marcus grinned. 'Yep. Terrorists would trade their own mother for this stuff.'

His eyes softened. 'Cate,' he began. 'I really wish there was another way. If I could get into that powerboat instead of you, you know I would do it.'

'It's OK, really. I'm the one small enough to stow away and I know the layout of *The Good Times*. It has to be me.'

Marcus tried to smile, gave up and patted her gently on the shoulder. 'Good girl,' he said quietly. 'When all this is over I'll take you for a slap up meal in Le Ricochet and I'll get Henri to pay.'

There was a short silence, then it was back to business.

'Don't try to be too smart,' he warned her. 'Don't waste time working on the computer security or trying to disable the external systems. Just go straight to the radar and sonar centres, smash massive holes in them and pour the acid in.' He smiled grimly. 'Short of blowing up the bridge with a missile, I guarantee you there won't be a quicker way of crippling that boat. Oh, and speaking of which, if you can disable the missiles as well that would be great. We'd rather not have them whizzing past our ears.

'Once you've done that, let us know and we'll be there with you. We'll have you off that boat in seconds, I promise.'

Marcus's words echoing in her ears, Cate looked at her watch. Quarter past eight. She only had another five minutes of cover left.

She carefully lifted the hatch up a few centimetres above her head and peered out into the launch area. It was dark and empty. Tass and the bodyguards were nowhere to be seen. Silently, Cate pulled herself up through the hatch and slithered on her front to the edge of the mini harbour. Still no one. Keeping her head low she moved swiftly along onto the lower deck, watching for any guards that may have been posted there. But all the men seemed to be upstairs, no doubt deciding whether they could enter into a full-scale fight with the still swooping helicopters.

She paused, taking her bearings and trying to work out the quickest way to get up to the bridge and the radar and sonar centre without being spotted. It was far too risky to take the lift, Cate decided, opting instead to run up the metal staircase.

She reached the top deck and hid behind a small metal pillar, trying to work out where everyone was. The helicopters were no longer buzzing around the yacht but they were still close enough for the searchlight to pick them out in the black sky. *No markings*, thought Cate approvingly as she watched the choppers circle the yacht from a distance.

In front of her, the swimming pool glistened serenely amidst all the mayhem. It was hard to believe that, only the day before, Cate was sitting around it relaxing with the children. She forced herself to concentrate, remembering what Mikey had said when they first arrived on the boat. The pool, then the bridge which held the sonar and radar control and behind that the missiles. Through the sporadic light of the flares and the spotlights of the helicopters, Cate could see into the bridge room. She made out silhouettes of figures too dark to recognise.

Running from pillar to pillar in the moments of darkness, Cate worked her way along the deck. She had a near miss when a guard silently flitted past her as she paused behind one of the lifeboats, but he was too intent on looking upwards to see her. Now she was by the bridge and she had a clear view through the door. One man was at the centre of the activity, pointing at dials, giving orders. It was Bill.

Now, more than ever, Cate knew she had to be careful. Tass, Mikey, even Ahmed, she felt she had a good chance against.

But Bill, he frightened her. Really frightened her.

Moving slowly and silently, she lifted herself on top of the bridge unit, praying Bill would hear nothing above him. She crouched between the radar mast and missile launcher.

She remembered Marcus's parting shot as she had left the galley that evening. 'KISS,' he had said. 'Don't forget to KISS.' Keep It Simple, Stupid. She smiled to herself. Straight down the barrel of each of the missiles then. She slipped off her left trainer and unscrewed six of the studs, one for each missile, and carefully poured them down each of the launch tubes. The whole job was done in less than twenty seconds but already Cate could smell the liquid begin to burn away at the missiles.

Hoping that would do the trick, Cate slipped down and peered inside the bridge. There were only two men in there now. Bill seemed to have vanished – gone down to the security centre perhaps.

One of the men was wearing headphones, facing away from her and poring over a bank of screens. The other was close to the door with his back to her. There would never be a better chance.

She whistled and the guard looked over his shoulder out through the door. Cate whistled again and he left the doorway and walked curiously on. As he passed into the shadows, she launched a kick into his stomach. As he fell forward, winded, she came behind him, using his momentum to push him head first over the safety barrier at the top of the stairwell. As he pivoted on his stomach there was no air for him to shout. Cate bent down, lifted up his shoes and heaved him down the stairs, his body thudding down to the darkness below. She ran down the steps and surprising herself with her strength, dragged his inert body into the shadows.

Cate paused for a minute, regaining her breath. With adrenalin coursing through her veins she had turned into a fighting machine, aggressive, powerful, ruthless even, almost as if it was someone else rather than her. But she had no time to analyse her feelings now, there was work to do.

She pulled out her gun from the rucksack and rested it against her left hand, her right hand on the trigger, and moved silently back to the bridge.

'What the hell—' It was the last words the guard said for a good few hours. Cate hit him hard over the head with the gun, and his body slumped onto the desk behind him. She grabbed a clump of his dark, curly hair, lifted it up and checked his eyes. Definitely unconscious.

She got to work, with no idea when the next guard would appear. She searched frantically for something indicating the radar and sonar computer system, checking above and below the desk and on the shelving which ran around the room. Cate cursed aloud. Of course, she remembered now. What José had said as she had walked past the bank of screens downstairs on the bottom deck. 'The sonar system,' he had told her proudly, 'is here.'

Cate groaned. Now she had to do what she could to retrieve the situation but it was taking a lot longer than she had imagined.

She grabbed her phone and texted Marcus. *Pull back until I say so.*

Immediately he was back to her. *We are getting you off now.*

No can do. Sonar and radar still not down. Will call you. Trust me. She turned to leave the bridge, moving silently in the darkness of the deck. As she left the confines of the small room she breathed deeply, taking in the sharp night air. Then she felt something cold and hard pressing into the small of her back.

'Welcome aboard, Cate Carlisle,' said Bill.

Down in a corner of the bottom deck, Cate sat on a chair, staring angrily at Bill, Mikey and Ahmed who were standing in a semi-circle around her. Bill was going through her rucksack, pulling out objects and throwing them onto a table next to him.

'A gun! Jesus, Cate, what the hell are you doing with a gun? And a knife. And what's this?' Bill had found the survival tin and was picking through the contents, trying to work them out. 'OK, Cate, talk to me. I'm hoping you can give me a really good reason why you were on this ship at night, trying to sabotage our bridge and at the same time carrying a gun, because it looks really bad.'

'I could say the same about you, Bill,' said Cate.

For a few seconds Bill was shocked into silence. He swallowed hard and tried again. 'Who are you working for, Cate?'

'You first, Bill.' She knew she was winding him up but she couldn't help herself. She desperately wanted to know why Bill was involved, wanted to hear what he had to say, but there was only more silence.

Ahmed walked up to Cate and slapped her hard around the face, so hard that she nearly fell off the chair. She turned back to face him and was taken aback by the hatred she saw blazing in his pale eyes. 'I thought she was trouble from the first time I saw her.' He turned to Mikey who was standing expressionless, not taking his eyes from Cate's face. 'There was something not right about her. Too sharp, too nosy, always watching and listening and being in places she shouldn't be. I told you, Bill.'

'You've been a really stupid girl.' Mikey spoke at last. 'How're we going to sort fings out now?'

'We could kill her,' Ahmed suggested helpfully. 'Chuck her over the side.'

'Hang on a minute, Ahmed.' Mikey was alarmed. 'She's only a kid. We can get her to talk easily and then just dump her somewhere when all this mess is over.'

Bill was silent, considering the options. 'No need to panic,' he said finally. 'She'll be our insurance, our ticket out of here. She's got a gun and high tech equipment. She's not working alone. I'll ask you again, Cate. Who are you working for?'

'No one.' Cate was playing for time, frantically working through the possibilities for escape. Cate knew that if she stayed the likelihood was that she would be killed, if not now then very soon. She had nothing left to lose, she had to try to escape.

'I came out here because I saw the animals yesterday and I wanted to rescue them.'

Ahmed hit her again and this time Cate did fall off her chair. She landed painfully on her ribs, her face throbbing, and stayed there until Mikey picked her up and stuck her roughly back on the chair.

'If you came on your own, where did the helicopters come from?' Ahmed demanded.

'Don't know.' Cate was spitting out blood. 'Nothing to do with me. I thought it was some of Tass's flash mates playing tricks.'

The three men were looking at each other, none of them willing to make the final decision. Cate saw her chance. She darted between Mikey and Bill and, before they could put out a hand to stop her, she was running for the rear of the boat and the stairwell. Halfway up the stairs she felt a hand grabbing at her foot and, turning sharply, kicked out hard at Ahmed's forehead. He groaned and fell backwards into Mikey who shoved him roughly aside before following Cate up the stairs.

She was heading for the sea-level deck and the safety of the water. She reached the top of the stairs, running out towards the mini harbour and up ahead of her she could see the outline of the power boat, and next to it the jetskis floating free in the water.

She felt hope rise in her. Just a few metres to go, and as long as the jetski started first time she would be away. She could hear the shouts of her captors behind, they were gaining on her. Heart pounding with the effort, she raced out from the tunnel, the fresh air hitting her like a wall. She was just about to take a huge leap onto the jetski when she heard a noise behind her. Instinctively she turned and felt something shoved hard over her bruised face. Then everything went black.

CHAPTER 17

'Well, well,' said Tass. 'And just what new and amazing species do we have here?'

From her position sprawled at the bottom of the cage, Cate stared blearily upwards taking in the expensive shoes, the tanned legs and finally the faces of Tass and Lulu.

She feigned surprise. 'What's going on? What I am doing in this cage?'

'Yeah, yeah, Cate, nice try.' Tass sounded calm and relaxed, amused even. 'Well, who'd have thought that a kid like you would end up causing us all this trouble? Don't worry, Cate, we'll soon have you out of there. But not just yet.'

'I would enjoy being in that cage if I were you, Cate Carlisle,' Lulu hissed happily at her. 'Where you're going, this will seem like the lap of luxury.'

'Hang on, wait – please.' Cate dragged herself upright to face them, swaying as she hung onto the bars for support. She forced herself to meet Tass's eyes. 'People will be looking for me – my friends, my family. If I don't call them soon then they will know something bad has happened.'

'Oh?' Tass sneered, his handsome face contorted with hatred. 'How scared am I?' He looked down at his clunky gold watch. 'Two hours ago, when you were enjoying a nice sleep, *The Good Times* left Antibes harbour. In roughly ten minutes she will be out in international waters and then it doesn't matter who your friends are. If they try to mount any misguided rescue attempt we will be completely within our rights to use maximum force against them. We will send them to the bottom of the sea.'

For the first time since she had come to, Cate was aware of the deep throbbing sound of the engines vibrating along the floor of her cage. Her heart sank. It was all too late.

'Where are you taking me?' she asked.

This time Lulu answered her. 'Well, we were going to have a press conference somewhere nice and civilised like Venice or Monaco. But now, thanks to the trouble you have caused us, we are having to relocate to Sibya. As it happens, Tass is very friendly with the head of the Sibyan army. They don't like spies there any more than we do.'

Now Cate was really beginning to panic. She knew about Sibya, she had heard her father discussing with colleagues about how the small East African country was one of the most dangerous places in the world. Once people crossed the borders, they often disappeared without trace.

'My father will never stop searching for me.' Cate was trying to sound confident, keep calm. 'He knows so many people around the world, you'd never get a minute's peace.'

'He can't prove anything.' Lulu smiled at her benignly. 'Not really. No one can. The thing is, Cate, you've been far too good at covering your tracks. We'll just deny everything. We'll say that the last time we saw you was on *Catwalk II* and no one will be able to prove otherwise. Will they, darling?' She looked brightly at Tass, who nodded his head approvingly.

'And,' she continued, her smile becoming more menacing by the second, 'they'll never know that we've been thinking about extending our research to humans. And you'd be the perfect specimen to start with.'

Cate went cold. These two had clearly lost all semblance of humanity and rationality. They were scary, very scary.

Tass smiled at Lulu lovingly.

Cate looked from one to the other, the shock registering in her face. 'You two?' she said incredulously. 'You two are – you two are together? An item?' She was laughing now through her fear – she couldn't help herself.

Lulu turned back to her crossly. 'We're married – husband and wife. We've been together for years. We met at school.' Her face softened. 'I wasn't rich enough so we had to keep it secret from Tass's vile father. Tass couldn't risk being cut off from the money, you see.'

Tass looked sadly at his wife. 'I'm sorry, darling. I still feel really bad about that.'

'It's OK,' Lulu said brightly. 'I understand. I wanted the money too.'

'But now,' Tass said gleefully, 'now, I'm going to prove myself once and for all with this amazing, genius breakthough.

220

Presidents, scientists, businessmen. The whole world will be begging me to work with them.'

'It wasn't *your* breakthrough!' Cate was outraged, her sense of justice getting the better of her. 'I think you'll find that the professor came up with the knowledge.'

It was a mistake. Immediately Tass's mood changed, his face darkened as one strong hand came through the bars grabbing at Cate's arm and pulling her closer. She stared at him, half terrified, half fascinated, wondering how she could have ever thought him handsome.

'You – know – far – too – much.' He spat it out, his spittle landing on Cate's face. 'In ten hours we reach Sibya. Then you are . . .' He ran his finger across her throat. 'I will take personal pleasure in telling the good Colonel there to make your life one long, lingering hell.'

As the doors closed behind them and the overhead lights faded to a dull gleam, a shaken Cate took stock of her situation. It was grim, she knew that. Any hope she had of persuading her captors that she was just a silly teenager caught up in something beyond her comprehension was long gone. She had seen what had happened to the professor when he became a problem. She shuddered. Part of her was angry at herself for being so stupid as to think that she, Cate Carlisle, could possibly have succeeded in taking on, and winning against, such determined thugs. Undeniably too, she was terrified of dying, of the actual process of being killed, of never seeing her friends and family again.

But still, she wasn't ready to give up. She looked around at her surroundings. The bars of the cage were spaced at ten centimetre intervals, far too close for her to squeeze through. She couldn't see where the lock was but, looking at the other cages around her, she spotted a digital box situated right at the top of the doors. But even if Cate knew which code to punch in – which she didn't – a quick attempt convinced her she wouldn't be able to reach the box anyway.

There was a rustle in the cage next to her and, turning to look, she saw a pair of eyes staring back at her. As her vision adjusted to the gloom she saw a tiny panda, no more than thirty centimetres high, big black circles surrounding his frightened eyes.

Opposite her, in a large cage, she could just make out the outline of a white tiger cub, its yellowy eyes watching her carefully. In the next cage, a small black mass had crammed itself into the far corner of the cage, its long arms wrapped protectively around its chest. *A gorilla*, thought Cate. *A beautiful mountain gorilla.*

She counted around twenty cages, all full of animals who should by rights, she thought, no longer be babies and should be roaming safely in protected reserves. She pictured their parents, imagined the heartbreak they must have suffered as their babies were torn away from them and she felt tears prick at her eyes.

Now they were trapped here, manipulated and experimented on by monsters, and would never be allowed to mature. No doubt they would become some sort of freak show, objects not of beauty and strength but of curiosity, to be sold to the highest bidder as if they were sacks of grain.

Cate was furious now, her anger energising her. She patted her clothes and her pockets. She had been thoroughly searched and everything removed from her. Even the laces on her trainers had gone. But her trainers hadn't. Remembering the CCTV camera clicking overhead, Cate crept to the back of her cage and looked at the bottom of her trainers. Relief washed over her. The studs were still there.

Just then there was the sound of footsteps in the antechamber. The doors opened, the lights came up and a ginger-haired man walked in holding buckets of food and a heavy, pointed stick.

'Feeding time at the zoo.' The accent, the voice was familiar. Suddenly Cate was aware of a thin face peering at her through the bars.

'Oh. I thought it was you.' It was the guard who had found Stripy for her the day before. Was it really just a day ago? She could hardly believe it.

'You got me into a lot of trouble, kid. Well, you stuck your nose in where it shouldn't be and look what happened to ya.' He whistled cheerfully as he stood up. 'Now it's your turn to be in a whole heap of trouble.'

Cate watched as he began to feed the animals. They were clearly waiting for their food, but even so they didn't rush to the door. She soon understood why.

The guard opened the door of the panda cage next to her and without any preamble gave the baby a sharp thwack across the back of its neck with his stick. The panda shuddered but didn't howl, just lay cowed and subdued, crouched as far away from the guard as possible.

'Hey!' shouted Cate, horrified by what she was witnessing. 'Leave him alone, you coward.'

'You want some too?' The guard was back at her cage, his stupid face peering through the bars at her. 'A hiding would do you the world of good, I reckon. It's like these animals. They may be precious but they still need to know who's boss and I think you do too.' Before Cate could move, the door was open and she felt a sharp pain across the back of her calves.

'Next time it's your feet.' The guard grinned. 'Hurts more there.'

Cate groaned, rubbing her already swollen legs. She couldn't believe that someone so young could be so vicious. But she had learnt her lesson. *No more mouthiness*, she thought. *Action next time*.

From the back of her cage she watched carefully as her tormentor went about his work. As the guard clicked the code on each of the cages, Cate quickly realised that it was the same one. And one she could easily remember. 181542 – the battle of Waterloo plus the number of the bus she got to school. Thanks, Ginger.

Just as the guard was about to leave the room, Cate called out to him. 'Please.' She forced herself to sound weak and close to tears. 'Please can I have some water, something to eat. I'm so hungry, so sick.'

He came back to her, delighted at her pleading. 'I might do, I might not.' His grinning face was tantalisingly close. 'It's not like you're precious like these animals, is it, darlin'?'

Cate felt like grabbing his head and smashing it against the bars. *Not yet*, she thought.

'OK, kid. Here's the deal. I think you need just a little bit more time to think about all the trouble you've caused. I'll bring you something to eat when I'm ready.'

I'll be waiting, thought Cate.

As soon as the door closed she went to work. She moved away as far as she could from the overhead cameras and felt down to the bottom of her right trainer. She unscrewed the first stud she came to and poked her fingers into the hole. First time lucky. She pulled out the tiny vial and slid it under the palm of her hand. As smoothly as possible she rolled onto her stomach, her head facing the bars where they met the back wall.

She took a deep breath, unscrewed the vial and poured a few drops of liquid onto the bottom of each of the three bars that lay in the shadows, hoping against hope that it would be too dark for the camera to see what she was up to. There was a slight smell of burning, a soft crackle and, before her eyes, Cate could see the metal dissolving as if it was a stick of sugar rock.

Cate gave it a few seconds then pulled hard at the bars. They moved inwards into the cage. She looked at the hole, checking it out for size. Easily large enough for her to slither through.

Now she needed a weapon. She poured what was left of the acid over one of the loosened bars and cheered inwardly as a section fell onto the straw with a dull thud. Now all Cate had to do was wait.

The guard was clearly in no hurry to feed her. Hours ticked by and Cate fought to stay awake. The animals around her were still, but she saw by the glimmer of their eyes that they were awake and watchful, unnerved no doubt by her unfamiliar presence.

Then she heard footsteps and sprang into action. She slipped quietly through the hole, picked up the heavy bar and was by the side of the door just as the guard came through it. She swung hard and hit down with a ferocious anger she didn't know she possessed. The man slid silently to the floor, the electronic door swooshing shut behind him.

Within seconds, Cate had dragged him into an empty cage and pushed him to the back, covering him with straw. She quickly ran her hands over his skinny frame and found a small Glock pistol which she slipped into her pocket. Then she turned to the animals which were up at the front of their cages, staring at her in astonishment.

'I'll be back for you, I promise,' she said quietly as she passed through the door and out into the next room.

She had to get to a computer and fast. Clearly the ship had managed to avoid the IMIA search parties, otherwise she had no doubt that Marcus would have already sent in a rescue team. Or perhaps they knew exactly where *The Good Times* was but were holding back, fearful of causing her death. In that case, they couldn't know that the boat was heading to Sibya, because if it reached there, she'd have no more chance of escape. She had to somehow alert Marcus and get the ship stopped.

She crept quietly to the exit and opened it slowly. She had banked on Ginger being the only guard on duty at this time of the night but, to her horror, she realised she had miscalculated. Wandering up and down the corridor, presumably waiting for his mate, was a short but very square, black man who looked as if he was more than capable of taking care of himself.

Cate shut the door again, her heart beating hard. She had a

loaded gun but knew she had to save her bullets if she could and, in any case, was not sure she could bear to really use it on another human being. She could try to attack him with the bar, but what if he managed to call for help before she had time to use the computer? Then she remembered the blue laptop. She was down on her knees in an instant, scrabbling at the tiles as she tried to pinpoint the hiding place. She found it and to her utter relief the computer was still there.

She brought it out and stuck it on one of the work surfaces that ran around the room, praying that there would still be life in the battery. It was dead. She looked wildly around her and then back into the hole in the ground and kicked herself for panicking. The lead was there. She plugged it in and the computer screen flickered into life. She willed it to hurry, to load up before the second guard realised that his mate had been gone for too long.

As the screen lit up, Cate almost wept with happiness. The internet sign was glowing, she was connected to the outside world again and, after the last few lonely hours, that felt amazing.

Relief washed over her as she saw the computer had Skype. With trembling hands she logged into her account, clicked on Arthur's number and pressed dial. The tone rang loudly in the small room and Cate jumped nervously, waiting for the guard to come rushing in. But even though it was four in the morning in London, within seconds Arthur was on the line.

'Sis,' he said. 'Thank God. Where are you? We've been going demented here. Dad and Monique are on their way to the South of France, raising merry hell with everyone they can think of. Dad's even woken up the Foreign Secretary and the French Prime Minster has sent in their special forces to find you.'

'Wow,' said Cate, impressed. 'Didn't know Dad had those sorts of contacts. Where are they, then?'

'Umm, the problem is that the IMIA have lost you,' said Arthur. '*The Good Times* must have activated its radar shield.'

Cate thought for a second. 'Arthur, listen. Call Marcus now and tell him we're headed down the North West coast of Africa to Sibya.'

Arthur grunted anxiously. 'Cate, I don't like the sound of that.'

'The missiles have been disabled, but not the radar or sonar,' said Cate. 'And I'm down at the bottom with the animals. But I won't be able to hold the guards off for much longer.'

'OK, sis,' Arthur's voice was scared but determined. 'You can rely on me.'

'I know,' Cate said. 'And Arthur . . .'

'Yep.'

'I really love you, you know. If anything happens.'

'It won't, sis, I promise. Now go and hide, stay safe whatever it takes. I promise you the cavalry is on its way.'

The line clicked and Arthur was gone. There was nothing she could do now except what Arthur had said: try to stay safe and pray that her brother would be able to get her location to her rescuers. But although she had sounded brave, the reality was scarily different. She knew that it could take hours for the search party to locate *The Good Times*.

Suddenly she heard banging on the door. 'Bobby Joe? You

in there, big fella?' There was a pause.

Cate crept to the door and shut out the light, gripping the gun tightly in her hand. The knocking started up again.

'OK, Bobby Joe, quit messing. You're worrying me now.'

Cate silently opened the door. She felt his hesitation and then slowly he stepped inside the door. In an instant, she had the gun at his back. 'Keep walking,' she said. 'Keep walking. All the way to the zoo.'

'Whatever you want, miss,' he said. 'Whatever you want. I don't want to die.'

She left the guard in a cage, tied up with some baling string she had found in the straw and with his shirt stuffed in his mouth.

She hesitated, looking around at the animals. Then she went from cage to cage punching in the code, checking that the doors were unlocked. *Just in case I need to get them out in a hurry*, she thought.

Cate ran back to the antechamber, and felt the ship shudder as it suddenly swung round. She grabbed the laptop to stop it from sliding across the worktop and braced her legs against the floor.

Cate ran out into the corridor, her heart pounding. Should she take cover in the bottom deck or would she be safer up on the top deck? Suddenly she heard a thump and felt the ship quiver as something flew overhead and landed with a heavy splash in the water not far from the boat.

Cautiously, she went up to the main deck, knowing instantly she needn't have worried about being spotted. In front of her was utter chaos. At the desk, three men were frantically looking from screen to screen whilst around them a troop of guards were standing by, waiting for direction, orders, anything.

Suddenly Bill appeared at the far end of the deck. 'Get up on deck,' he screamed at the assembled men. 'We're under attack.' As the guards rushed towards him the boat shook and swayed.

They've found me! Cate thought, with relief. *And that was a direct hit!* She was horrified but thrilled.

Then she heard the unmistakable and wonderful sound of helicopters, dozens of them, followed by the crackle of bullets and the high frequency ping as they hit the hull.

Cate ran through to the now empty room and took the stairs three at a time. The top deck was lit up with searchlights from the choppers piercing the early morning gloom, and guards were running around taking aimless shots into the sky above them. There was no sign of Tass or Lulu and no one seemed to be giving orders.

Then, from above, Cate heard a voice booming through a loudspeaker. 'This is the French Navy. Put down your weapons and surrender or we will open fire again.'

Bill appeared from the bridge, his blond hair standing out against the searchlights. He was carrying a gun and his face was distorted with rage. He shouted furiously at the guards. 'You useless morons!' His voice rose over the clamour of the helicopters. 'Man the missiles. The missiles!'

No one moved. The guards were staring upwards, hypnotised by the lights of the helicopters. Then Bill ran from the bridge to the missile stand. Screaming at the guards to help

230

him, he rotated the tubes so that they were facing up into the sky. Then, dodging a hail of bullets from above, he ran back to the safety of the bridge and pressed a large red button.

Nothing happened. Bill thumped the button again. Then he brought his fist crashing down on the button again and again and again. As he did, Cate saw dark figures appearing at the open sides of the helicopters and men began shimmying down ropes to the smashed and shattered deck. Suddenly Marcus was at her side, his white teeth shining at her through his balaclavad face.

'Thank God, Cate,' he said. 'I thought we'd lost you. If you hadn't gone online to Arthur we'd never have been able to track you down.'

Ignoring the men in black that were now disarming the guards and handcuffing them, Bill was still on the bridge, trying in vain to fire the missiles.

'Shall you tell him about the acid or shall I?' said Marcus gleefully.

'You can,' said Cate, grinning. 'He doesn't like me any more.'

She looked around her. The gunshots had finally stopped, all the guards lay flat on the deck, handcuffed.

'Tass and Lulu.' Cate felt sick. 'Marcus – Tass and Lulu, where are they?'

Marcus spoke into a walkie talkie. 'No sign of them. We've secured the entire ship.'

The bottom deck, thought Cate.

She suddenly ran for the stairs, Marcus following behind her. 'Cate,' he said, 'Cate, where are you going?'

'The animals!' Cate ran down the stairs and back through the deserted bottom deck. She reached the security door and charged through. A French SAS officer was standing guard by the computer desk where the guards had been sitting just a few hours earlier.

'Have you seen a man and woman?' Cate panted in French.

He shook his head. '*Non*. No one.'

Cate pushed past him into the open secure room and then flicked the switch. Marcus watched in amazement as the wall moved aside to show the glass door.

'God,' exclaimed Marcus. 'What's behind here?'

'The animals!' Cate was almost shouting now. 'This is where they keep the animals.' She ran through and stopped suddenly. The cages which had held the smaller animals had been removed from their racks, the doors to the larger cages were wide open. Cate saw, with a sinking heart, that some of the leashes used on the animals were missing as well.

'They've taken them,' she said helplessly. 'They're gone.'

She sank down to her knees. 'I knew he wouldn't let them go,' she said, looking up at Marcus. 'They're all he needs to build another life.'

But Marcus wasn't listening. 'If he didn't get them past my guard, then he must have got them out another way,' he said, hunting along the walls. 'There must be an escape route somehow to somewhere.'

'The submarine bay.' Cate was up on her feet now. 'Behind this wall is the submarine bay.'

She ran back out to the corridor and looked at the screen. The instructions were there. *Open Door One, Open Door Two.*

She clicked on the second option but the shutters stayed stubbornly still.

Outside hatch opening, flashed up on the screen. *Access to submarine bay denied.*

'Oh my God,' said Cate. 'He's taking them in the submarine.'

Marcus spoke grimly. 'He won't get far. We'll have a torpedo on it as soon as it leaves the boat.'

'No!' cried Cate. 'The animals are on board. They'll die with him.'

Marcus spoke to her gently, trying to reason with her. 'Cate there is nothing more we can do.' He put his arm around her shoulder. 'We can't let him get away with those animals. What they have there is amazing, but it has the potential to be incredibly dangerous in the wrong hands. You know that. What if they use their research on more animals, or on humans? We simply cannot allow that to happen and, if that means destroying the submarine, then we'll have to do it.'

She stared back at him, trying to absorb what he was saying.

'Cate, sometimes we have to make hard choices.' Marcus looked at her with sadness in his dark eyes. 'This is one of those times.'

'No!' Cate was shouting now. 'There has to be another way.'

Suddenly she remembered what José had said to Oak. 'If the inner door is open, the outer hatch will not open. Otherwise the whole boat will flood.'

'I've got it,' she shouted to Marcus and the men standing behind him. 'Get that shutter up and the outer submarine hatch will come to a halt. Come on, we've still got time.'

Marcus stared at her and then charged down the corridor, his men following. Cate was there first, her hands under the bottom bars of the shutters trying frantically to prise them up.

'Here.' A tall soldier behind Marcus ushered her to one side. 'It's locked. Stand back.' He brought a gun from his side and shot along the base of the shutter. Then all five men crouched down and put their hands underneath the now free bar and began to push upwards.

The shutter still didn't move.

'Try harder,' screamed Cate. 'Come on, move it.' She could hear the roar of the submarine's engines getting louder as Tass built up power in the engines. The men strained and pushed but nothing happened.

'It's no good,' said one. 'It's locked tight.'

Suddenly Cate remembered the bar she had left in the side room. It was still there standing against the wall where she had left it. She ran back down the corridor and handed it to Marcus. 'Here,' she said. 'Use this.'

He pushed the tip of the steel bar under the base of the shutter and, sweat pouring off his brow, pushed down hard on the other end. Another man joined him, then another and slowly, slowly the shutter began to move upwards.

'It's working,' shouted Cate. 'You're overriding the system.'

But now ice cold sea water was sloshing around their ankles. 'The hatch is already open,' Marcus said. 'We're too late.'

Just then the shutter heaved upwards and Cate and the men ducked beneath it and into the submarine bay. The submarine was already nosing out towards the hatch, waiting for the last few seconds when the door would fully open and it could leave.

'If that hatch keeps opening, this ship will go down now the inner door's bust – and we'll all go with it!' Marcus shouted in Cate's ear above the noise of the submarine engines. 'Cate, you have to run for it. Leave it to us.'

'No,' said Cate. 'I promised myself I wouldn't give up on the animals.'

'Cate Carlisle,' said Marcus, grabbing her by the shoulder and turning her back towards the door. 'For once, just do as you are told.'

The water was now knee high and rising fast. The boat took a sudden lurch and leaned over to one side. Marcus pushed Cate towards the shutters. 'Go!' he said.

Then, suddenly, miraculously, the shutter shot up in the air. And at the same time Cate saw, as if in a dream, that the outer hatch had stopped its upward climb. In fact, she could hardly believe her eyes. It was now closing up again.

'How on earth did that happen?' Cate looked at Marcus in disbelief. He shrugged, looking as shocked as she was.

'I dunno,' he said, as soldiers swarmed around the submarine. 'I honestly thought we were in for a night swim.'

Piot appeared behind the men, wading towards them down the corridor, looking very pleased with himself. 'I had no idea I was that good with computers,' he said, giving Cate a hug. 'Somehow I managed to switch the hatch instructions from open to close. I am very proud.'

'Did you have to do it with a hand grenade?' Henri was behind him. 'Honestly Piot, sometimes you are so heavy-handed. You've made a terrible mess.'

Tass and Lulu were out on the landing bay, Tass trying hard

to explain himself to the nearest guard, Lulu glaring viciously over towards Cate.

'The animals!' Cate started to wade towards the submarine.

'All OK,' shouted one of the soldiers, poking his head out of the submarine hatch. 'Alive and well, although rather smelly.'

'Speaking of which, Cate . . .' Marcus was looking at her with a strange expression on his face. 'I don't mean to be offensive but, well, you could really do with a good, long shower.'

EPILOGUE

'It's not fair, really, it is *such* a downer.' Nancy was sitting at the far end of the long wooden table, moaning to Monique who had had the misfortune to be placed next to her by an expansive and beaming Pierre.

'I've lost my captain, my PA *and* my boyfriend,' she said, lighting up yet another cigarette. 'All in the same afternoon. I mean it's just outrageous. I feel like going to the papers about it. They're always writing about what a wonderful easy life I have flitting from party to yacht to premiere. If they knew how much I've just been through — '

'No!' Marcus, who had been doing his best to ignore Nancy for most of the meal, couldn't help himself. 'Nancy! We've talked about this. Henri debriefed you, Cate's dad has spoken to you, we all have. The events of the last week didn't happen, remember? You didn't have a captain called Bill and your PA has suddenly taken up another job with an oligarch in the Ukraine. And as for Tass, well romances come and go.' He grinned. 'If you speak about this to anyone, we'll have to kill you.'

Nancy gasped in horror before she realised that Marcus was joking.

'Seriously, Nancy, forget this ever happened. Think of it like . . . like that tummy tuck and breast enhancement operation you had done last summer in Harley Street. Gone, forgotten, never spoken of again. Pouf.' He snapped his fingers and took a swig of wine.

'How did you know about that?' Nancy was outraged. 'No one knows about that.'

Marcus grinned happily. 'And so it shall remain. Unless of course . . .'

Nancy subsided into a sulky silence but soon cheered up when Monique kindly began asking her about her modelling. Cate looked around the table happily. Her dad had finally finished lecturing Henri about putting his daughter in danger and was now chatting to Wendy about cricket, his face animated as they discussed the merits of the last Ashes tour of the UK. He had already given Cate and Arthur the biggest telling off of their lives, although Cate could tell that secretly he was rather proud of his offspring. To her left, Piot was entertaining Arthur with tales of his computer genius and Arthur was doing his best to keep a straight face.

Every so often, Arthur's hand would creep sideways to give Cate's arm an affectionate squeeze, and it was all she could do not to give her brother a bear hug every time she looked at him.

'You know that Arthur is the real hero in all this,' Cate had told everyone at least five times as they flew on Nancy's pink helicopter from Antibes to St Tropez for a celebratory lunch.

And now, along the table lay the remnants of what had been one of the best meals of Cate's life. Someone must have told Pierre it was a special occasion, and even by Le Ricochet's high standards it had been historic, Pierre and his waiters bringing an endless series of exquisite tapas – deep red chorizo baked in Spanish rioja, glistening lemon and garlic chicken, seared pork brochettes topped with emerald parsley and silvery-grey marinated sardines crammed into their dish.

'You're not leaving us as well, are you?' Wendy asked Cate, dipping some bread into the sardine dish. 'We've got a new captain coming tomorrow and Nancy is throwing a party on Friday. That lead singer everyone's talking about is coming. She's definitely got her eye on the drummer. I heard her telling Jules all about it. Look's like it's business as usual.'

'I wouldn't dream of going back to England yet,' said Cate. 'I'm looking forward to a summer having fun with you guys. I think we've earned it, don't you?'

The older girl smiled and nodded. She was still sad, Cate knew, at finding out the truth about Bill. Wendy stood up and wandered down to the beach with Nancy to play with the children.

'What will happen to them – to Tass and Bill and Lulu?' Cate leant over to talk to Henri as he carefully pulled a prawn apart and popped the meat into his mouth.

'The thing is, Cate,' he sighed, his hard face softening, 'in our line of work, justice isn't always that straightforward. We can't just put them on trial, well, not the sort of trial you would imagine, because we simply can't have everyone knowing about us, about you, about what Tass and Lulu were up to.' He shrugged. 'Sometimes you have to keep things quiet. Imagine if people knew that there was something that could technically bring an end to ageing. Without careful planning, the consequences could be horrendous.'

'Where are they now?' Even as she asked, Cate didn't really want to know. Actually she wanted to forget all about the last few days and simply enjoy the sensation of being alive in such a beautiful place with all her favourite people around her. But she had to ask, otherwise she knew she would never get any peace.

'Right now Tass and Lulu are in a holding jail, sitting in an island off the coast of Africa,' said Henri. 'Even Tass couldn't buy his way out of there.'

'And then?' Cate asked anxiously. She couldn't work out why she was so worried about such vile people, but she was.

'Cate, whatever you do, don't feel sorry for them,' he said grimly. 'A few hours more and you would have been lost forever. Most likely they would have killed you without compunction, without mercy.'

Or experimented on me, thought Cate, shuddering, suddenly cold in the warm sunshine.

Her father looked up, eyeing her anxiously from across the table, trying to decipher what Henri was saying to his daughter.

'Tass's father is a very powerful man with contacts around the world.' Henri was choosing his words carefully. 'He has been on to the French President and we believe he has already been lobbying the White House. Cate, we have to expect that Tass will be released sooner rather than later. But from what I hear, his father will have him under such close control that he will never be able to cause any mischief again. Lulu, though, has no powerful relatives and Tass will have no choice but to do what his father wants. He won't be able to help her. She won't see freedom until she is too old to remember how to spell the word.'

Cate sat quietly for a minute. 'So he gets off scot-free and she pays the price,' Cate said. 'How is that fair?'

'It's sort of fair. Lulu was the one in charge,' Henri said. 'She was the brains behind this. She set up Nancy and enlisted Bill and corrupted the professor with talk of power and respect and, of course, money. Without Lulu, none of this would have happened.'

Cate thought back to the darkened rooms, the cages and the horror of the damaged beaten creatures. 'How are the animals?' She hardly dared ask.

'Don't worry, they're doing well,' Henri replied. 'They will be looked after for the rest of their lives.'

'Will they grow old?' Cate asked.

'Who knows?' Henri said quietly. 'Maybe the effect will be short-lived, and nature will find a way of fighting back.

Either way, you saved countless other animals from a dreadful fate.'

'And Bill?' Cate asked quietly. This time her father spoke.

'I'll tell her Henri,' he said, casting a warning glance in the chief's direction. 'Cate, Bill didn't make it off the boat.' Her father was talking to her gently, watching her face for signs of distress. 'He died in a final shoot out. He and Mikey and Ahmed. They didn't want to surrender.'

'Oh,' said Cate, swallowing hard. 'I'm sorry. Did you ever find out who he really was?'

'Henri is still trying to unravel his story,' her father explained. 'We know that Bill had been using his cover as a yacht captain to work for all sorts of dangerous people. We're trying to locate a family to tell them that he is dead, but perhaps we never will. Perhaps he didn't have a family.'

Cate was silent. She looked at her father and Arthur, at Monique who had come up to her end of the table and was crouched down by her side holding her hands comfortingly.

'It's OK,' she said finally, touched by their worried expressions. 'It's OK. I know how lucky I am.'

Her mobile rang. She looked at the screen and Cate's heart leapt. 'Michel,' she said, answering it. She got up from the table and wandered off to the far end of the garden. 'Michel, I am so, so sorry about the other night. I was kind of . . . busy.'

There was a pause. Cate held her breath.

'It's OK,' he said. 'It does me good to be stood up by a beautiful girl now and again. But don't make a habit of it, OK?'

Cate smiled. 'I promise I won't,' she said. Her heart soared. So there was going to be a next time.

'Was it anything important?' asked Michel curiously.

Cate looked back at her friends and family sitting around the table in the warm French sunshine, the sea sparkling behind them, the promise of a long fun-filled summer ahead of her.

'It was,' Cate said happily, 'but it isn't any more.'

ACKNOWLEDGEMENTS

A massive thank you to everyone who helped with this book.

To Brenda Gardner at Piccadilly for believing in Cate Carlisle enough to sign her up, Ruth Williams, who kindly held my hand through the edit and my agent Elly James for being brave enough to take me on in the first place.

My friends – both young and just a little bit older – aka the 'focus group', sadly too numerous to mention, who read, advised and cheered me on. Your support has been incredible.

A special, huge thanks to my wonderful sons George, Conrad and Lucas, my keenest, yet kindest critics and a constant source of inspiration and fun.

And finally and most importantly, to my husband Graeme, whose love, endless encouragement and patience has gone way beyond anything I could reasonably have expected of him. Thank you doesn't even begin to cover it.

The **CATE CARLISLE** Files

DEEP WATER

ISLA WHITCROFT

When sixteen-year-old Cate Carlisle receives an
invitation to spend Christmas in Australia with her
boyfriend Michel, she drops everything to join him.
Michel is helping out in a remote turtle sanctuary run by
passionate eco worriers, but as Cate soon discovers,
sinister forces are at work and now both animals
and humans are in grave danger of destroying each other.

Cate needs all her quick wits, plus the help of her
computer geek brother and her glamorous friends
to prevent an eco catastrophe.

The exciting sequel to *Trapped.*

My So-Called Afterlife

TAMSYN MURRAY

*'Aaargh!' Stumbling backwards, the man's face
flooded with horrified embarrassment. 'How long
have you been standing there?'
My mind fizzed furiously. He could see me.
He could actually see me! I could have hugged him!
Well, I couldn't, but you know what I mean.*

Fifteen-year-old Lucy has been stuck in the men's loos
since she was murdered there six months ago
and Jeremy is the first person who's been able to
see or hear her. Just her luck that he's a seriously
uncool geography-teacher type – but at least
he's determined to help.

Once he's found a way for her to leave the loos,
she's soon meeting other ghosts, including the
gorgeous Ryan. However, when Jeremy insists
that she helps him track down her killer, she has
to confront her greatest fear . . .

THE BEX FACTOR

Simon Packham

When Bex gets an audition for
The Tingle Factor, she begs geeky
guitarist Matthew to accompany her,
hoping he'll lift her performance.
But the judges want Matthew – not Bex!

Bex swallows her envy, and persuades a reluctant
Matthew to take part by offering to help with his family.
While Matthew gets swept up in the world of reality TV,
it's Bex who has to deal with his sweet,
affection-starved sister and his angry, disabled mother.

Warm, thought-provoking,
and very funny.

Heartbeat Away

LAURA SUMMERS

Becky's getting stronger by the day after her heart transplant, but soon she starts to have disturbing experiences.

Vivid pictures of unfamiliar people and places suddenly flash through her mind. What can they mean? Mysteriously drawn to a park on the far side of town, Becky begins to unravel a mystery deeply buried in her new heart.

Dark Ride

CAROLINE GREEN

*A shiver crawled up my spine. It felt like the loneliest place
in the world. For a second I thought I caught a snatch of
music in the air, but it was just the wind whistling through
cracks in the fairground hoardings.
My instincts screamed, 'Run away, Bel!
Run away and never return!'
But instead my fingers closed around the ticket in my pocket.
ADMIT ONE.*

Bel has never met anyone like Luka. And the day she
follows him into the abandoned fairground, she is totally
unprepared for the turn her life is about to take . . .

piccadillypress.co.uk

Go online to discover

☆ more exciting books you'll love

☆ competitions

☆ sneak peeks inside books

☆ fun activities and downloads

☆ and much more!